東京
トーキョー

G H O U

T O K Y O

グール
喰種

SUI ISHIDA
SHIN TOWADA

DESIGN. Shawn Carrico

TRANSLATION. Morgan Giles

Library of Congress Cataloging-in-Publication Data

Names: Towada, Shin, author. | Ishida, Sui. | Giles, Morgan, translator.
Title: Tokyo ghoul (Tōkyō gūru. English) -- original story by Sui Ishida ; written by Shin Towada ; translated by Morgan Giles.
v. 1. Days -- v. 2. Void -- v. 3. Past
Description: San Francisco, CA : VIZ Media, LLC, [2016] | Series: Tokyo Ghoul light novels book series
Identifiers: LCCN 2016032597 | ISBN 9781421590578 (paperback)
Subjects: | BISAC: FICTION / Media Tie-In.
Classification: LCC PL876.O78 T65 2016 | DDC 895.63/6--dc23
LC record available at https://lccn.loc.gov/2016032597

Published by VIZ Media, LLC
P.O. Box 77010
San Francisco, CA 94107

Printed in the U.S.A.

10 9 8 7 6 5 4 3 2 1
First printing, April 2017

www.viz.com

VIZ SIGNATURE

ORIGINAL STORY BY
sui ishida

WRITTEN BY
SHIN TOWADA

TRANSLATED BY
Morgan Giles

cast of characters

TOUKA KIRISHIMA

A female Ghoul. Nicknamed “the Rabbit” by the CCG and considered dangerous. Goes to school and has friends.

AYATO KIRISHIMA

Touka’s brother. Executive in Aogiri Tree. Up-front about his hostility toward his sister, but he can’t quite rid himself of all feelings for her.

YOSHIMURA

Manager of Anteiku, a café where Ghouls gather. His behavior is very mysterious. And his real identity is…

KEN KANEKI

A boy who received an organ transplant from a Ghoul. Now a human who eats other humans. That conflict is now his driving force.

HIDEYOSHI NAGACHIKA

Kaneki’s friend since childhood. Passionate. Working for the CCG now.

RIZE KAMISHIRO

Ghoul nicknamed “the Binge Eater” for her frenzied feeding habits. Kaneki received a transplant of one of her organs.

KAZUICHI BANJO

Former leader of the 11th Ward, who was in love with Rize. Weak, but admired by his subordinates.

AKIRA MADO

CCG investigator. A genius who graduated at the top of her class at the Academy.

KUREO MADO

Akira's father. A veteran investigator, abnormally obsessed with Quinques.

NISHIKI NISHIO

Ghoul boy. Student in the pharmacy department at Kamii University.

KIMI NISHINO

Nishiki's girlfriend. Knows that he is a Ghoul.

ENJI KOMA

Works at Anteiku. Said to have once been a very ferocious Ghoul.

KAYA IRIMI

Works at Anteiku. Leader of the Ghoul organization Black Dobers until she started working in the café.

東京喰種

TOKYO GHOUL

[PAST]

TABLE OF CONTENTS

T O K Y O

東京

[PAST]

喰種

G H O U L

#001 DIFFERENT KIND

The road where I wished we'd always be together was the road where we parted ways.

The simple wish to live is a crime in this world.

We are overwhelmingly more powerful than humans, yet the only existence we're allowed is one that must be hidden from their eyes.

We are Ghouls.

Each Ghoul experiences countless bitter interactions with people—some dramatic, some trifling—and Touka Kirishima was no exception.

When she was young, Touka's family was betrayed by a human who had taken care of them, and the memory of being chased by an investigator from the Commission of Counter Ghoul, the agency that seeks to exterminate Ghouls, was still fresh in her mind. That is why she and her brother Ayato both lived with their backs turned to humanity.

"How stupid can these bastards be, fighting us when they're so weak? Eh, sis?"

Dispassionately, Touka and Ayato looked down at the twitching body of a man on the pavement, splayed like a suicide who had jumped from the top floor of the building above.

"Shit . . . shit . . . you little punks! I'm a Futamaru leader, meant to control this area! I . . . can't get killed by some brats!"

Ayato raised an eyebrow at the man, who still had enough life in him to groan in anger.

"Cool it, Ayato," Touka cautioned him. "He'll die soon. All this action's got me hungry. Let's go eat."

Touka started walking away. Ayato seemed unconvinced, but he followed after Touka in resignation.

But then the man mustered his last bit of strength to get up.

"This'll . . ."

He released his Kagune again.

"You little brats! Ah!"

His thought seemed to be to get them while their backs were turned.

But at the same time the siblings' Kagune emerged from their backs, Rc cells surging through them. They fixed their red eyes on the man.

"You moron."

"At least die like a grown-up."

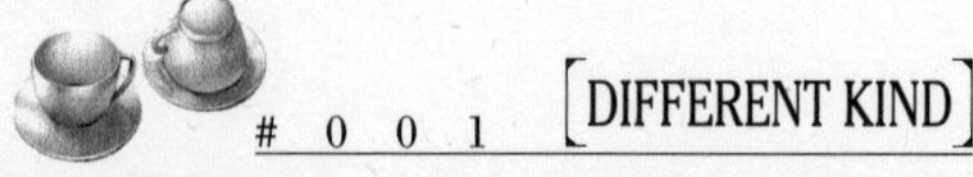

Their Kagune punched through him and, with one last cry, his life was snuffed out.

The world of Ghouls is eat or be eaten. With strength on your side, there are very simple structures that allow you to live without being trampled on by others. It is a very different world from the one humans live in, with their boring, stifling rules.

But there are some downsides.

The color started to return to Touka's bloodred eyes. She looked up at a nearby apartment building. Light was pouring out of the windows of one apartment, and she heard joyous laughter. *All these people are nothing but Ghoul bait, and somehow they go on living with no sense of crisis.* She felt disgust welling up in her at their lack of awareness, and a scene from long ago came to mind.

It was of the three of them—Touka, Ayato, and their father, Arata—around the time when they were living under the pretense of being humans. And within this memory was the same sense of peace as the happy family behind those brightly lit windows . . .

But Touka shook her head, flinging those memories far away. *Ghouls and humans are not the same. There's no overlap*, she told herself, and turned away from the light.

II

"'Ghouls rule Tokyo?!' huh . . ." Touka read the headline from the cover of a magazine that had been left on the apartment floor. *Something he stole, I suppose.* Touka set the magazine on the table and sighed.

It was already past noon. Ayato was perhaps still asleep, because he hadn't come out of his room yet. Touka debated for a little bit before calling for him.

"Ayato," she said, in the direction of his room." I'm going over to Mr. Yoshimura's place. What are you doing?"

No response. *Either he's asleep or he didn't hear me.*

"Ayato?" She tried again.

"Shut up. I'm not going . . ." His voice was full of irritation. The door jerked open and Ayato, who looked like he had just woken up, walked out into the living room. He ignored Touka as he combed his hair.

"What's with the attitude?"

Touka sounded irritated too, and Ayato looked at her blankly. He looked away and sat down on the sofa, picked up the magazine that Touka had just set on the table and started flicking through it.

"Go whenever you want," he said.

Before, he'd followed her everywhere she went, but now he only acted on his own whims. Everything Touka said seemed to rub him the wrong way. *I never know what he's thinking.*

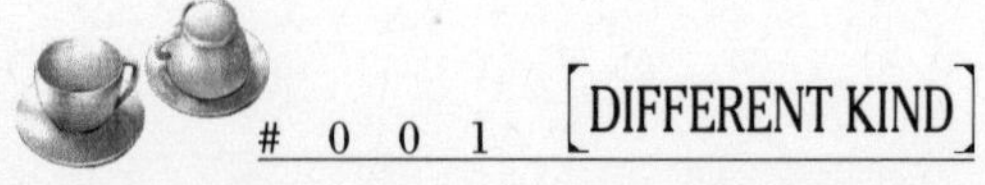

When she arrived at Anteiku—from outward appearances a normal coffee shop, but in actuality the headquarters for the Ghouls of the 20th Ward—the café was quiet, perhaps because it was after lunch-time. A few people were having coffee, but they all appeared to be Ghouls.

"Welcome . . ."

Yoshimura, the manager, was drying cups in the back of the shop. He noticed Touka and looked her way. He already seemed to know about the Ghoul that had died in the fight with Touka and Ayato. Preparing herself for the usual lecture, she took a seat at the counter and asked for a cup of coffee.

Yoshimura said nothing as he made the coffee and set it down in front of Touka. She had expected a warning from him, but his silence actually made her feel more uncomfortable. This was far crueler than she had anticipated. Feigning calm, Touka brought the coffee cup to her lips.

"Yomo dealt with his corpse for you, but if you keep this up the CCG will start asking questions."

And there it is. He just jumped right in.

"This again," Touka said and turned her head, still holding her coffee cup.

"The other side has ways of identifying Ghouls from the marks left by Kagune. They will find you if you get too cocky. And by 'you,' I don't just mean you, Touka. I mean Ayato too—"

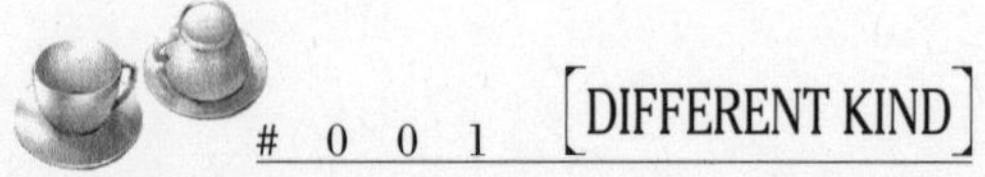

Just then the door chimed. A new customer had arrived—a human.

It was strictly forbidden to talk about things that would identify them as Ghouls in front of people. Yoshimura returned to his work as if nothing had been going on, and Touka closed her mouth too.

Another human customer came in, then another. Ayato preferred to shy away from Anteiku, and this strange environment was probably the reason. Human customers in a Ghoul café. A place where Ghouls and humans coexisted, albeit temporarily. This seemed to grate on Ayato's nerves.

"Ayato's so young, but he has tremendous strength. I worry that that strength will take him in the wrong direction," Yoshimura said, quietly, so that people could not hear him.

"What's the wrong direction?"

"If you have power, you have a lot to lose."

Yoshimura always came back to these vague lessons. Annoyed, Touka set her coffee cup down on its saucer roughly.

"Touka."

Saying nothing, she walked straight out the door of the café and did not look back. As she walked away, she thought she could almost hear Yoshimura sigh.

With the sun shining and people bustling here and there, the city was full of life. But Touka's heart was sinking. *Go home*, she whispered to herself, and started walking again, but time after time she came to a stop. Looking at her reflection in a store window, she saw an expression frozen on her face. *I can't go back looking like this.*

After checking to make sure there was nobody around, Touka ascended to the roof of a nearby apartment building, using walls and low roofs as footholds. Up there she had a nice view, but it was windier than down below, and Touka's black hair whipped around her.

I'll just stay here until I calm down. Touka sat down on the edge of the roof, wrapped her arms around her knees, and closed her eyes.

But she soon heard someone crying somewhere. At first she tried to ignore it, but the sound continued, and she began to listen closely. The crying seemed to be coming from somewhere below the building. Touka looked down, searching for the owner of that voice.

"A kid . . ."

A boy, about five years old, was sitting there crying. Listening carefully, she heard him saying, "Mama." *He got separated from his mother, perhaps?*

"Right, now, where is his mother?"

None of the people near him appeared to be his mother. Those passing by looked down at him wondering what was wrong, but they all walked by without saying anything. He was curled up in a little ball, sobbing, "Mama, mama."

For some reason, Touka saw Ayato when he was little.

Clicking her tongue at herself, Touka came down from the roof in a way so as not to be noticed. *Why do I always get involved with humans like this?* she thought, then called out to the boy from behind.

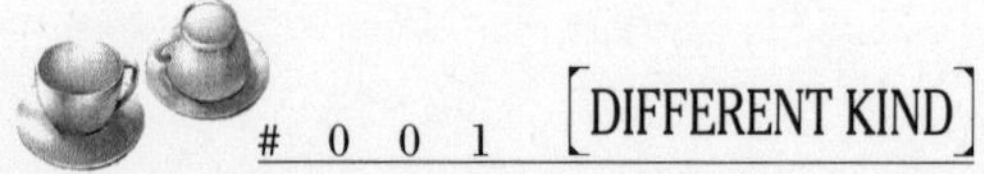

"What's wrong?"

The boy jumped with surprise, then turned to look. He stopped crying at once.

"Where's your mother?" she took the opportunity to ask.

"Waaaaaah!"

The boy began to sob again, sparked by Touka's question.

"Wait—"

Suddenly all the passersby looked at Touka. *I must seem very suspicious right now.*

"Oh, you idiot, come here," she said, grabbing his hand and pulling him away from there.

The boy seemed to calm down as they walked. They went into a nearby park and sat down on some deserted swings. The boy started swinging happily.

"What—what's going on?"

The thought suddenly came to her: *Maybe I should just leave him and go.*

As she considered her options, the boy said, "Thanks."

"Huh?"

"Daddy told me I should say thank you when somebody helps me," the boy told Touka, who was lost in confusion.

"But I haven't helped you . . ."

Touka didn't know what to say, but the boy kept swinging happily, seemingly satisfied now that he'd thanked her.

"Where's your dad?"

When she'd asked about his mother, he'd started crying, so she

decided to try asking about his father.

"At work!" he said, cheerfully. Suddenly he stopped swinging, crestfallen at the realization. "If I don't go back to kindergarten, daddy's gonna be mad."

"Kindergarten?"

He must've run away.

"Then let's take you back."

The boy silently picked up a pebble from the ground near his feet and threw it toward the fence surrounding the park, sulking.

The easiest thing to do would be to take him to the nearest police station. But Touka was the right age to be in school, too, if she were human. If she took the boy to the police, they would likely start asking prying questions about why she wasn't in school. *I should've never gotten involved*, she thought.

But then she heard a voice.

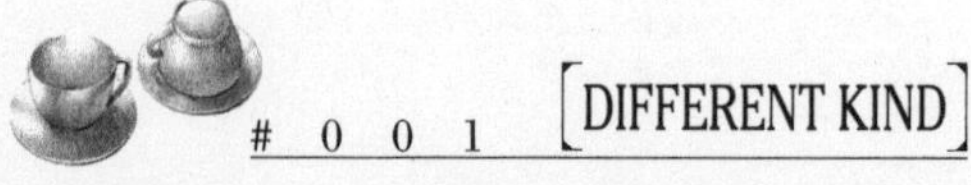

"Shota! Shota!"

Touka looked around and saw a man in a suit coming toward them.

"Daddy!"

Shota leapt down from the swing and ran toward him. *I guess that's his dad.* His father gave Shota a rap on the head.

"You made me worried!"

"Oh, I'm sorry!"

I guess that's that. All wrapped up now. Touka started to leave without saying anything, but she caught the boy's father's eye.

"You're here with my son, aren't you?"

"N-not really . . ." Touka stuttered.

The man smiled." He ran away from his school, we've been looking for him all over. Thank you." He was about the same age as Touka's own father. She felt a twinge of nostalgia.

"I think he was looking for his mother," she told him, meaning it in a kind way, but as soon as she said it, the expression on the boy's face changed.

"I wasn't! Don't make stuff up!" Although she'd been looking after him until now, the boy started yelling. "She's lying!"

Touka didn't know what to do, but the man started rubbing his son's back. "Of course," he said in agreement. *What a naughty boy.*

After telling her she was mischievous, the father thanked her, saying, "I'm sorry," and left the park with the boy in his arms.

Left alone in the park with a stupid expression on her face, Touka muttered to herself, "What was all that?" *I went out of my way to help him and that's the thanks I get? His parents must've spoiled him rotten.*

I never should've gotten involved.

Touka kicked the ground in frustration, then left the park.

III

A week passed. Touka was off to Anteiku in search of coffee again. She'd asked Ayato if he wanted to come along, but he had shouted, "You don't have to tell me every time you go out, you know! I don't care!" and that was the end of that.

When Ayato went out without saying anything and didn't come home for hours, Touka got worried that something had happened. So she told Ayato where she was going thinking he shared the same concern, but apparently he did not. And that difference made Touka's heart hurt.

If I were a human would I have to suffer like this? She looked up and saw two boys around high school age.

"I got this album and the lyrics are just awesome, you gotta hear it!"

"Is this the one that's all in English?"

"Yeah! I translated some of the songs so if you don't understand it, I can just sing along!"

"Oh, uh, that's cool, dude, but . . ."

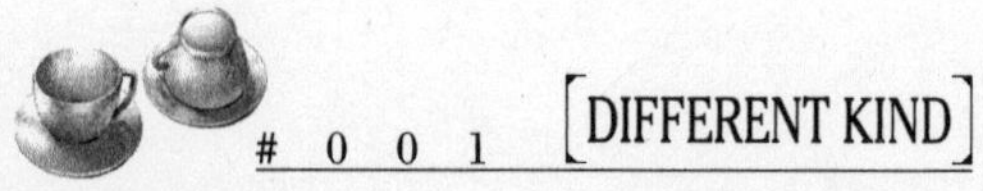

Look at them, nothing but smooth sailing under sunny skies. Never had to struggle a day in their lives. Touka felt a deep envy and hatred in her heart.

"Hey, you're the . . ."

Suddenly, someone called out to her. She looked and saw a man in a suit on his way back from work. She recognized him from somewhere. After a moment's thought she realized that he was the father of the boy she'd found crying.

Once she recognized him, she became cautious. Touka remembered how he'd believed what his son said, and she wondered if he was going to try to have a word with her.

But the man did not seem hostile. In fact, he smiled broadly.

"I just wanted to say, I'm sorry about troubling you before. I got a call about Shota running away from school, so I went out looking for him with his teachers. Thanks for staying with him in the park."

The conversation could have ended there. Just when they both should have said their goodbyes, the father said, "One more thing. You said he was calling out for his mother?"

Touka was still distrustful, but neither could she stand being completely misunderstood.

"He was sobbing and saying, 'Mama, mama,' " she said bluntly.

"I see," said the boy's father, looking worried. His attitude seemed very different from before. "I guess he tries not to say anything in front of me, but he must be missing her."

Touka frowned at these meaningful words, and the man forced a bright expression.

"My wife passed away six months ago."

". . . Oh."

"He's very good when he's with me, but at school he's starting to act out. He runs away, like he did this time, or he starts fights . . . He hates it when he hears people at school talking about their mothers."

And here I thought he was living innocently and happily with his family. This unexpected confession brought to Touka's mind an image of the boy crying for his mother. A shot of pain ran through her. When she'd seen him crying it had reminded her of Ayato when he was little, but suddenly Touka could see something of herself in him too.

When Touka had lost her mother, she'd cried like that. And her father had comforted her.

"But he's still got to go to school."

The man smiled sadly.

"He doesn't want to cause me trouble, he wants everything to be 'normal.' It's his own way of getting through it and fighting on . . ."

So that's why he got angry when I told his father that he'd been crying for his mother—because he thought his father would be worried?

"Oh, I'm sorry. For telling you all this. But thank you. You're very kind."

Those last words were a phrase that Touka was not used to hearing. She raised her head in surprise. But the boy's father didn't notice. He checked his watch and suddenly looked hurried.

"Oh no, I said I'd be there early today, but I'm late now. I'll see

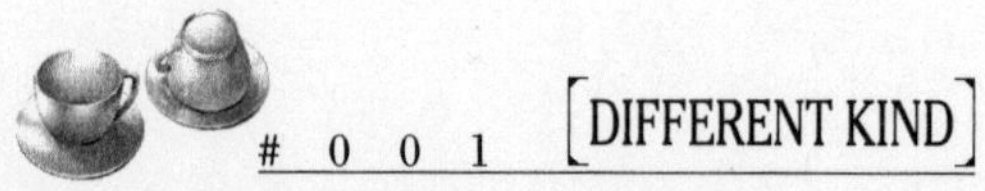

you around, I suppose. Thank you," he said, and rushed off to pick up his son. Touka found herself unable to move from the spot for a while.

That's why she didn't notice.

With the incident with the boy and his father's words echoing around her head, Touka went into Anteiku and, to her surprise, saw that Renji Yomo was there. Unlike Yoshimura, who generally accepted most things, Yomo's mere presence made Touka feel tense. She felt slightly uneasy knowing that he'd had to clean up the evidence when she and Ayato had gotten sloppy recently.

Sure enough, when Yomo glared at her, Touka felt uncomfortable and turned her head.

But Yomo's gaze was directed at something on the other side of her.

He walked past her without saying anything and opened the café's door. He cast his severe gaze left and right, then he spoke.

"You've been followed, Touka."

"What?"

She quickly gathered herself and looked around, only to see someone running off. From the way the figure carried itself, it appeared to be a Ghoul.

"We were just talking about you."

Yoshimura's face stiffened. He looked at Touka.

"Some friends of the Ghoul you and Ayato killed are aiming to retaliate against you."

Now Touka remembered that the Ghoul they'd killed had said he was one of the leaders of Futamaru, which ran things in this part of town. Although Anteiku was in charge of the 20th Ward, there were more than a few Ghouls that operated independently, but in groups. *I guess he was one of them.*

"They've already got Ayato."

"Got him?"

Ayato hadn't told her this, and she hadn't been able to tell from his behavior. But Yomo was not the kind of man to make jokes or tell lies. All kinds of things were happening without Touka realizing.

"You let your guard down too easily."

Yomo's warning made her blood start to rise.

"I haven't done—"

"Enough excuses," he cut her off. "You're asking for it," he said, then left the café. His words had been few, but Touka felt extremely chastised. Angry at not being able to respond, she started hitting the wall of the café.

"Touka."

"Shut up!" she roared, venting her anger, then rushed out the door.

"Dammit!"

I don't need to give some long speech, I can solve this myself. I can fight.

She looked around. The object of her bloodlust had disappeared into the distance, as if to say, *Come and get it.* Touka decided to take the invitation and headed in that direction.

But suddenly she felt anxious. Each battle set off a chain of

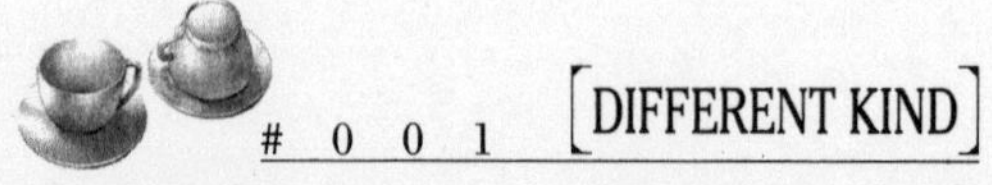

events with unexpected consequences. She wondered how long this would go on.

No, this isn't the time to think about that. Her senses were sharpened now, and her ears buzzed with a fierce cacophony of sounds.

It's not them. Not the ones who are after me.

"No way."

She stopped, frowning at the terrible voice she'd just heard.

"Daddy, daddy!"

It was that boy. He'd run away from school again, calling out for his dad as he fled. There was something urgent about his cries now, not like when he'd been crying for his mother.

But Touka turned away so as not to see him. Because he did have a father there to understand him and take care of him when he cried.

Unlike Touka. She had to fight to take care of herself, and she had no choice but to put her own life on the line to protect what was important. And right now, she had to take down the Ghouls who were trying to take Ayato's life.

The boy's voice eventually disappeared far into the distance.

At last the sun set, ushering in the time when Ghouls can operate freely. Touka stood at her own feeding ground. She could feel that something was wrong. Someone had invaded her feeding ground to provoke her.

Keeping vigilant as she moved, she walked into a back alley where there would be few passersby in hopes of luring her opponent in for the kill. But someone was already there.

"Kirishima, isn't it?"

The voice, colored with a hint of surprise, came from behind her. She turned to find a well-built man blocking her way out. She could see some other men behind him, taking the signal to come out of hiding. Four of them in all. They stood ready to attack her from all sides.

"You're the ones who've been following me?"

"That's right. You killed our friend, we kill you . . . That's the Futamaru code." A victorious look came over his face as he said the name of his group, the same one that the Ghoul killed by Touka and Ayato had mentioned. The four of them against one tiny girl on her own—there was no way they could lose.

But Touka looked them over dispassionately, then smiled.

"Your inferiority is showing."

"What?!" The veins on the man's forehead started standing out.

"You think it'll take four of you to take me. You know you're weak."

"What the hell do you know?"

"I know that you idiots came here to kill me."

"Shut it, bitch!"

Enraged by her words, the men released their Kagune. The one who seemed to be their leader had a kokaku to match his strong frame. Not a good match for someone with an ukaku, which deals

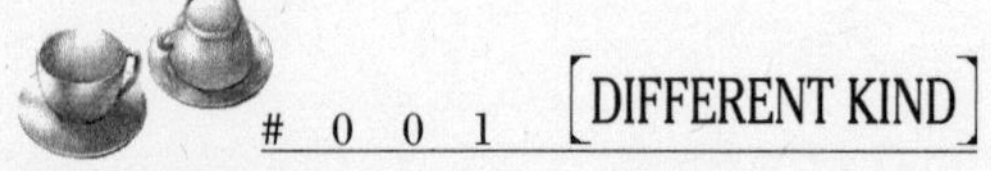

a light attack, but he attacked her directly so she was able to dodge him easily. The man who had been blocking her from behind disappeared, and just like that, their plan to surround her was over.

"What the hell . . ."

Her eyes still red, Touka put all her force into her back. Her throbbing ukaku instantly spread like wings, ripping through her clothes.

"With all of you in such a small space, it's like shooting fish in a barrel, you idiots."

It was so ridiculous she had to laugh.

Because the space was so narrow, Touka's ukaku could swing through all the men who lined the walls of the alley. There was nowhere to escape with them sandwiched in between tall buildings on both sides. They were all fair game.

"Aaaaaaghh!"

The man nearest to Touka took the first hit and staggered.

"Ugh!"

With one slash of her Kagune, Touka sliced the man's leg cleanly off. It spun in the air before falling to the ground with a thud.

He screamed in agony.

The giant man collapsed without the support of his leg, and his panic was palpable. His companions were also in shock.

Touka moved back to get some distance and immediately launched a long-range attack with her ukaku blade. The other three all had bikaku. Unlike their friend with the kokaku that could withstand her attack, these guys couldn't easily attack Touka from a distance.

“T-that’s unfair!”

“Hm? What is?”

Don’t push your luck, she thought, and laughed. One of the men, beside himself now, jumped out in front of the rest.

“Too bad, so sad.”

Touka focused her attack on one place: the man’s body. But he rushed forward wielding his bikaku, so Touka kicked off the wall, jumping high into the air, then used the momentum from her fall to split the man in two.

“Right, who’s next?”

It was all going Touka’s way. Her superiority was overwhelming.

“C’mon, take me!”

One of the remaining men turned his back and started trying to escape. *Nothing’s as weak as a man with a broken spirit.* Touka simply struck him as he ran.

Blam!

He crashed into the wall face-first, breaking his nose. He collapsed in a slump, losing consciousness quickly.

That left one man standing.

“Let’s finish this.”

The last man left was cowering in fright. He looked like he’d already lost the will to fight. It wouldn’t take more than a minute to take him down.

But then he yelled, “We have a hostage!”

His words stopped Touka dead in her tracks. *Hostage.* The first thing that came to her mind was Ayato. Seeing that Touka had

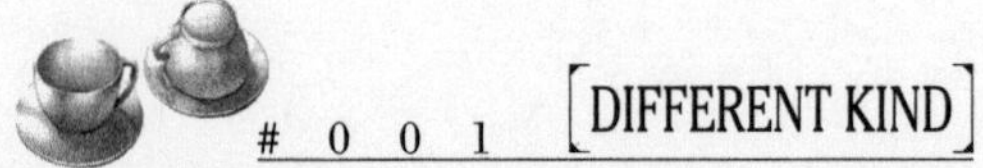

stopped and perhaps thinking that he could turn the tables, the man shouted, "I'll show you," before bringing out the hostage, who had been hidden at the far end of the alley.

Touka had another shock when she saw who it was.

It wasn't Ayato. It was a middle-aged man in a suit—that boy's father. He'd been bashed by these Ghouls, because his face was swollen, his clothes were bloodied, and he was drifting in and out of consciousness. It was clear that he needed to be taken to the hospital immediately.

"Why him?"

"You never talk to anyone but your family and the guys at Anteiku, but then suddenly here you are, being sweet to some humans. So I thought I'd keep an eye on him!"

They'd been keeping tabs on her all week. *So they know about the boy too.*

"We were gonna nab the kid too, but he ran away! Seems like it had an effect on you anyway . . ."

Touka was more than a little upset, as he said. *I never thought this man and his son would get caught up in my business.* There was one more thing. Her choices came to her now as sweat formed on her brow.

"When we asked him about you, he just said he didn't know anything! Oh, humanity—I mean, don't it just make you wanna cry? Right, don't move! We're gonna kill you, me and some other guys! Wait and see!"

He had the boy's father in front of him like a shield as he tried to escape. Touka's heart beat faster.

On one hand, there was the choice that Touka had to make in order to survive. That is, to kill this Ghoul and the boy's father...

"What are you doing, sis?"

A familiar voice echoed. Touka's head whipped around. There stood Ayato, head tilted to one side.

"Ayato..."

As she said his name, Ayato's Kagune emerged. He rushed forward, slicing through the air, and approached the man. His Kagune made a crunching noise as it took its form.

"Ayato, wait..."

She knew what she had to do. Unconsciously she let out a scream. But Ayato didn't hear her.

Bang!

At that signal, he brought down his Kagune, thick as an icicle and hard as rock. Ayato's Kagune went through not only the man who had attacked Touka, but also the boy's father. Touka gasped.

"Bunch of small fry. Boring."

Ayato kicked the body of the Ghoul he'd just killed.

"What's this human doing here?"

He looked like he was going to give the boy's father a kick too. "Stop!" Touka said sharply.

"What?"

She hesitated. "You'll get him too bruised to eat."

"Oh yeah."

Ayato put his foot back down, then looked around at the Ghouls

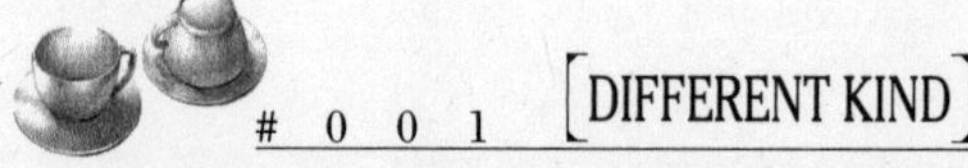

that Touka had killed.

"I came 'cause I thought it'd be interesting. How boring."

Having lost interest, he turned and started walking toward their apartment.

Touka stayed, staring at the boy's father.

Suddenly a shudder went through his body. *I thought he was dead.*

"Y-you're alive?"

The Ghoul who had tried to use him as a shield had, in actuality, taken the brunt of Ayato's attack, lessening the impact on the human.

But now, because of that, Touka had a decision to make.

There was no way he didn't know now that Touka was a Ghoul. *He knows my secret, I can't let him live. I have to kill him.*

Touka bit her lip and reached out toward the man.

"Daddy, daddy . . ."

But just then, in her mind, she heard the boy yelling. Crying and running through the streets. Still searching for his kidnapped father.

This boy who had already lost his mother would now lose his father. Just like Touka.

Touka pulled her hand back and pressed it to her face. All the heartbreak and suffering of the day she'd lost her father came back instantly as she imagined the boy. It was horrible.

Touka took a step back.

Although Ayato hadn't landed a fatal blow, the boy's father was still in serious danger. And this alley would have few passersby wandering down it until the morning at least. If she left him alone without helping him, he would certainly die.

It was a cruel, heartless choice to make. *But—*

If he's miraculously helped, then he might live.

If Touka took on that danger, then there might be repercussions.

She took a step forward, ready to make her escape.

Just then, she heard the crack of a stone hitting the ground and rolling away. She looked down at it and picked it up silently. Then, resolutely, she threw it down the alley, toward the main road. The stone ricocheted, and the sound echoed. This time, she left without turning back.

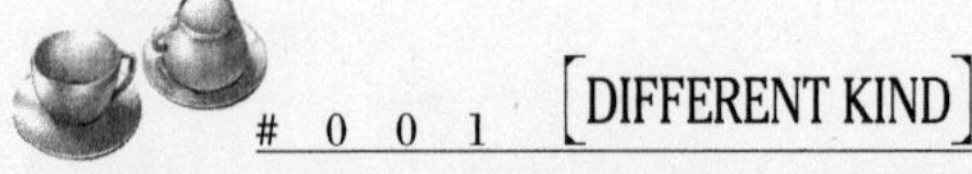

IV

Nothing changed in Touka's life after that. She had to imagine that the man had not been saved. If he had, then he would have told the CCG what had happened to him, and then their investigators would've started popping up all around her.

She felt the suffering that she had inflicted on that boy, who had now lost both of his parents. He would bear a grudge against her to be sure. Just like Ayato, who had been betrayed by humans and now hated them.

She could not push away this feeling as she walked aimlessly through the streets. *I want to forget, but the more I try, the more hold it has on me.*

As she walked, she heard the happy voice of a child, and she looked around. She saw some kids, about four or five years old, playing in the park. She realized she was subconsciously looking for the boy. *What are you doing*, she thought, and started to leave, but suddenly she overheard some mothers talking.

"Poor Shota . . ."

She stopped in her tracks. Shota—that was the boy's name. There must be tons of kids named Shota, but she kept listening, feeling strangely anxious.

"I know. But it's amazing what happened."

"It really is. I can't believe they found his father lying in the road."

Found his father lying in the road?

She jolted in surprise, clasping her hands to her chest to calm her thudding heart. Everything that had happened that night came back to Touka right away.

The boy's father, lying in a dark back alley. And there—

"Shota says that somebody told him where his father was. By throwing a stone or something . . ."

"Who knows what the truth is. But anyway, his father seems to be getting better now, so I'm glad."

She could almost see the boy noticing the pebble that she had thrown and running that way.

A vast range of emotions flooded through Touka. Before she could collect her thoughts, she muttered to herself, "Amazing."

This small, helpless human child, much weaker than Touka, had rushed there, sobbing all the way, but he didn't give up and he found his father. And saved his father?

I always stubbornly refused to believe that Ghouls and humans were similar. I could not admit it. But now I understand. Having love for your parents isn't a Ghoul thing or a human thing. It's something we share.

On the other hand, if he lived and was getting better, then why hasn't he told the CCG about me? Is it because he doesn't want the trouble, or is there another reason?

With all that she knew and all that she didn't know, she could not find the answer, no matter how much she thought about it. She wondered if her father, Arata, who had lived alongside humans, had seen this in them. *And if I get to know humans, like my dad, will I be able to see what he saw?*

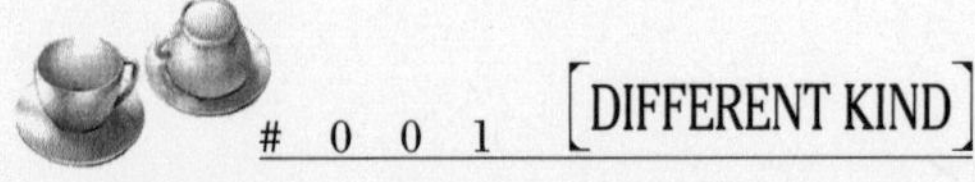

Her curiosity was rising, but there was no way of knowing—or there shouldn't have been.

"Touka, do you want to try going to school?"

Yoshimura made the offer to her after a conflict with Shu Tsukiyama, an eccentric and well-known foodie. The proposal came abruptly for Touka, but it was clearly something that Yoshimura had been mulling over for a while. He said that he could help with the entrance fees and documentation, as well as giving her a hand with studying.

"No way, old man," said Ayato, who preferred to keep his distance from humans. This was, perhaps, the right way to live for a Ghoul.

But however much you turn your back, humans are still there. And I live in the society that they built. So it might actually help me if sometimes I met people, got used to them, lived with them.

Besides that, she wanted to know. About humans. And about the world.

And someday I'll understand my dad, too, she thought hopefully as she slipped into her school uniform.

She didn't know that from now on, she would share joy that she could not find in the Ghoul world, as well as suffering that she might never have experienced otherwise.

"Ayato, listen to me. You won't believe what happened at school today. Yoriko was like . . ."

#002 SOLITARY READING

When a person is kind, that's enough to make them happy, my mother once said.

The loud buzz of his alarm clock hit his ears. He silenced it right away and got out of bed quickly. The morning light came in through the gap in the curtains, but the house was quiet. Nobody else seemed to be awake yet. He took a deep breath and went to the bathroom to wash his face and brush his teeth. When he got back to his room, he sighed with relief at the fact that he hadn't run into anyone.

Ken Kaneki was a high school sophomore. And he'd been living in the Asaokas' house—his aunt's house—for a few years now. But something about the atmosphere of the house did not allow him to feel at ease. *And maybe this'll go on for the rest of my life.*

He put on his school uniform, took his favorite book off the shelf and put it in his schoolbag. Suddenly he heard the house coming to life. It sounded like his aunt was awake. He heard her starting to make breakfast and yelling at the others to get up, and Kaneki left his room.

It was still a bit early to go to school, but the building would be open. As he crept quietly through the kitchen so as not to draw attention to himself, Kaneki saw his aunt. She'd arranged three place settings on the table. One for her, one for his uncle, and one for their son, Yuichi. Nothing for him. He didn't belong there.

He made it through the kitchen and paused by the door to put on his shoes. He felt desperate to get out of the house.

"Just how long are you going to sleep, really?"

Unfortunately his aunt came out into the hallway to complain. She looked around and saw him there.

Unlike Kaneki, who froze up, his aunt turned away in a huff and disappeared back into the kitchen, still shouting for her son. Kaneki pursed his lips and left the house, his shoes not yet laced up.

Kaneki had lost his father when he was four. And then his mother passed away when he was ten. Since then, he'd been living with his aunt, his mother's sister.

I don't belong there.

It was easier to believe that he himself was the cause of this searing pain he felt.

When he got to school nobody else was in the classroom yet, and he felt very free. He cracked a window, took out the pastry that he'd bought on the way, and started reading the book he had brought

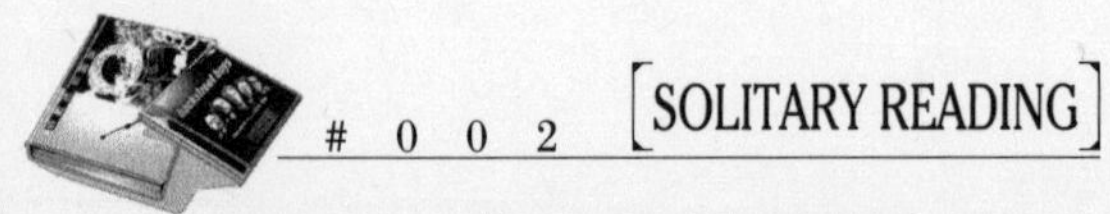

from home. The book was one that he'd seen his father reading long ago. His late father had loved reading, and many of the books on the shelves in Kaneki's room had belonged to him and now took their place as mementos.

He had no idea how much time went by. All he knew was that a gust of wind came in through the window he'd opened, flipping the pages of the book he was reading. When he looked up, he realized that his classmates were all around him, chatting away. *Everybody came in and I didn't notice.* Kaneki felt strangely oppressed in the happy, buzzy atmosphere. He looked up at the clock on the wall. It was almost time for class to start. His breathing quickened.

"Kaneki! Hey, Kaneki!"

The voice was cheerful. He looked up and saw Hideyoshi Nagachika, his eternally happy friend. Unlike Kaneki, who could often be found reading quietly on his own, Hide was the happy-go-lucky, outgoing, irrepressible type. Backpack slung on his shoulders, he headed toward

Kaneki, clutching a magazine in one hand.

"What's up?"

"What do you mean, 'what's up'? My favorite band's new album is finally coming out over here this weekend! I can't calm down!"

"Oh. They're from overseas, then?"

He slapped the magazine down on Kaneki's desk with a bang. It was a women's fashion magazine, one which most men would think twice about picking up. Kaneki was confused for a moment, but then he saw that there was a feature about Hide's favorite band.

"Look!" he said, opening the magazine and sticking it in front of Kaneki's eyes, so close it was nearly touching his nose.

"All right, calm down . . ."

Kaneki took the magazine from Hide and leaned back to take another look. *This article's a lot shorter than I imagined. Hide doesn't look like the kind to care much about details, but he's so passionate he collects little fragments of information like this.*

"Oh, and there's a really cute model in the spread about sandwich parties on the page before that one."

"Never let it be said you don't check every detail . . . Wait, what's a sandwich party?"

He smirked.

"Anyway," Hide continued, "I'm gonna go out and get it on the release date. I'm thinking I'll find it somewhere in the 20th Ward."

"What, nobody's selling it around here?"

"Nobody that's got the special posters and stuff! If I'm gonna buy it I gotta get the merch too. So, how about it? You coming with me?"

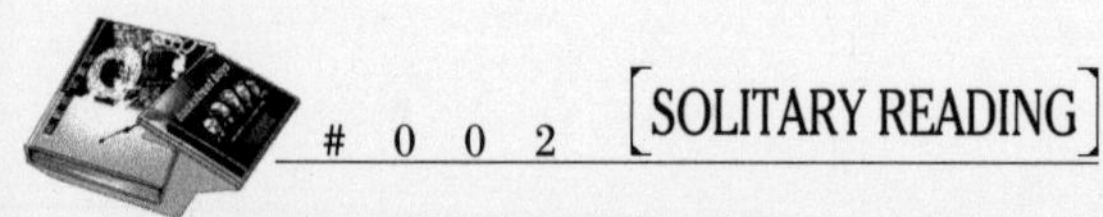

"Sure," Kaneki said. *Being at home on the weekends is exhausting.* After the cold reception he'd received that morning, Hide's invitation was very welcome.

"Did something happen, dude?"

Hide was surprised by Kaneki's quick response.

"No . . ."

"All right. I just thought . . ."

Hide tilted his head, looking into Kaneki's eyes. Feeling uncomfortable, Kaneki rubbed his jaw and said, "It's nothing."

"Right. Well, not long till the weekend. You better study up!"

He pulled a few more magazines out of his bag to go along with the one on Kaneki's desk.

"Wait, that's too much, man!"

Unfortunately, just then, their teacher came in. Kaneki looked at the clock—it was time for class. She didn't seem to have noticed him talking with Hide.

Suddenly a sentence came to Kaneki's mind. It was from "I Heard It in This Way," an essay by Osamu Dazai.

One needs no more proof that a man is not lonely than that he does not read.

When he had read that he'd felt, quite apart from whatever intention Dazai had when he wrote it, that Dazai had uncovered the reason why Kaneki read, and it shook him to his core. And the more he thought about how quickly the time passed when he talked to Hide, the more meaningful Dazai's words became.

But the knowledge and experience that books gave him were

the fuel that kept Kaneki going. And that made them irreplaceable friends too.

For now I have to read these magazines by the end of the week, Kaneki thought as he listened to his teacher speak.

When school was over, Hide dragged him into a fast food place, because he said there was still so much about this band he wanted to talk about. But Hide only talked about music for a little while; the rest was just random stuff. As they talked the sun went down, and Kaneki got back to the Asaokas' house much later than usual.

Talking to Hide had given him some distraction, but as soon as he got home his tension returned. He gave himself a few light pats to the chest to calm himself down before opening the door. He could hear the television on in the living room. *Probably my aunt.* He walked quickly to get to his room while her attention was elsewhere. But then the refrigerator in the kitchen caught his eye, and Kaneki stopped dead in his tracks.

That refrigerator was purchased with my mother's money.

He remembered how ceaselessly his mother had worked. And the reason she'd had to do it was for his aunt's family. *She was always bothering mom about money for one thing or another.*

That was not all. When his aunt's husband had gotten into debt and quit his job, his mother had taken on the burden for some reason and had to work more and more. *She worked herself to death.*

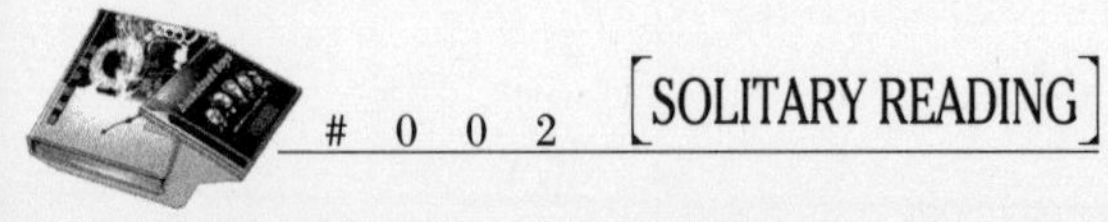

When I was a kid I thought my aunt must really be having a hard time, but now I'm not so sure what the reality was.

She lives in this two-story house. There's a big TV in the living room, with a huge white sofa and tons of plants. And that big, beautiful refrigerator is full of food. She kept begging my mom for money, but she was living better than we were.

A thick fog spread through his heart, one which would not dissipate.

He took a deep breath and tried to push the feelings away.

Mom always told me it was better to be the kind of person who gets hurt than the kind of person who hurts others. She told me that when a person is kind that's enough to make them happy. No matter what life threw at her she always met it with a smile.

Kaneki had a deep respect for his mother. He wanted to treasure the words she had left with him. Trying to nip those negative feelings in the bud, he decided to ignore those emotions. He raised his head high.

Standing before him was his aunt.

He was so surprised that his heart skipped a beat. Instinctively he took a step backward.

He couldn't hear the sound of the television anymore. She said she had decided to take a bath, and when she left the living room she saw Kaneki standing there. Overwhelmed by the urge to run away but unable to just ignore his aunt and leave, he was desperately scrambling for a topic of conversation when the weight of his schoolbag reminded him of Hide.

"Oh, uh, I'm going to hang out with Nagachika this weekend . . ." he said, mustering his courage. But as soon as he finished his sentence, his aunt turned and walked away.

"Oh." The sound escaped from his half-opened lips.

She turned around. "You know, when you're telling me things I couldn't care less about, you look just like my sister," she spat out, looking at him as if he were garbage. Then she turned and went into the bathroom. Kaneki's bag slipped from his shoulder and fell with a thud to the floor. His heart felt like it was going to break.

II

Although he'd hurried because he thought he'd be late, Kaneki actually arrived before they were supposed to meet. He grabbed a seat on a bench, took a book out of his bag and started reading.

"Hey, you're here early."

Unusually, Hide got there early too.

"You too."

"I've been waiting for this day for a long time! Did you read those magazines like I told you?"

Kaneki nodded at Hide, who was out of breath.

"Yeah, I read them. Over and over. I guess you'd like them back now . . ."

"Hold up, dude, they're too heavy for me to take them back now!"

"Which is what I thought, which is why I didn't bring them."

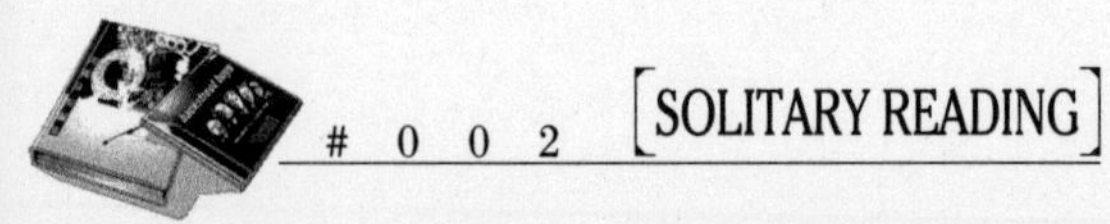

"Smart as always, man!" said Hide. Relieved that his judgment had not been wrong, Kaneki put away his book and stood up.

Next, the two of them got on the train and headed to the music store where Hide wanted to go.

"Fully stocked as always."

"Totally!"

Kaneki occasionally went to this music store with Hide. It was a small place but it had a huge range of CDs of all kinds, and you could tell they had a lot of love for artists.

Hide made a beeline to the CD he was after.

"Whoa, I finally got it!"

As he watched Hide, who was so excited about the CD and the bonus poster that came with it, Kaneki felt quietly envious. Hide's emotions were very clear-cut and he seemed to take a lot of enjoyment from life. Kaneki wondered what life would be like if he were like Hide.

"Man, I want to open it now!"

"Huh? No, wait until we get home."

"But I've waited so long already!"

Eventually Hide dragged him into a nearby café, where he sat down without ordering anything and gleefully tore at the plastic wrap like a child. Not knowing what else to do, Kaneki ordered a black coffee for himself and a cappuccino for Hide, then looked up at the TV hanging on the wall of the café. Hide was busy reading the lyrics from the CD's insert.

"Do they give a Japanese translation for the lyrics?"

"No, just English."

He squinted at the lyric sheet. Their coffees arrived, and Hide drank his cappuccino in one gulp before looking back at the insert.

"Do you understand the lyrics?"

"Mm, sort of."

Hide's better at English than he seems. He loves music in English so much that he started studying so he could understand the lyrics, but now his hobby is all-consuming.

Kaneki took a sip of his coffee and pulled his book out of his bag, so as not to disturb Hide.

"I think I'm gonna cry . . ." Hide said, a few minutes later, putting his hands to his eyes. He seemed to have finished doing the Japanese translation.

"Are the lyrics that good?"

"Yeah, but I just realized again that the album's finally here, and it got me all emotional again . . ."

"Right . . ."

I've never seen him look this happy, Kaneki thought. A fleeting glance at the TV caught his attention.

" . . . ward is also thought to be a Ghoul-related incident, but . . ."

"Ghouls are at it again, huh?" Hide muttered.

There are creatures in this world that eat humans, and we call them Ghouls, but despite the nonstop news about them, I've never gotten the chance to see one.

"There are guys whose job is to exterminate Ghouls, right? So what happens when they put themselves out of work?"

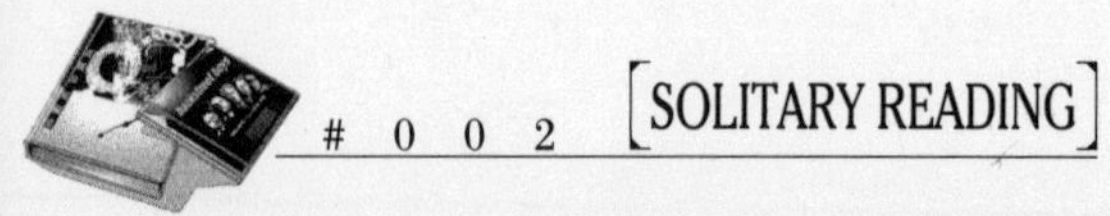

"But these Ghouls are superstrong, man. And they're supposed to be pretty hard to track."

"I guess that's why they need pros."

When he thought about the victims, a spark of anger ran through him. *The world would be better off without such dangerous creatures.*

"You never know, man, there could be 500-foot-tall Ghoul and humanoid robots battling it out somewhere every night for all we know."

Hide's thoughts were, as usual, on their own track.

"Hide, you're too old to be watching that kind of crap."

"I don't anymore! I mean, I used to . . . I just think giant robots are really cool!"

"Sure, dude," Kaneki laughed.

Hide bit his lip, hesitating. "I mean, you're one to talk."

"Me?"

"That book. Takatsuki whoever, that writer you like."

Kaneki loved reading, but his favorite author by far was Sen Takatsuki, who was often called a genius of the horror-mystery world for her masterful writing and the precision of psychological detail in her works.

"I mean, there are monsters in those books, right?"

"No. Takatsuki depicts the ugly side of humanity in a vivid, realistic way, and although there are some characters called 'monsters', they are still humans, not . . ."

"All right, all right! I'm sorry I said anything!"

Hide stopped Kaneki just as he got started. *I guess he thought I*

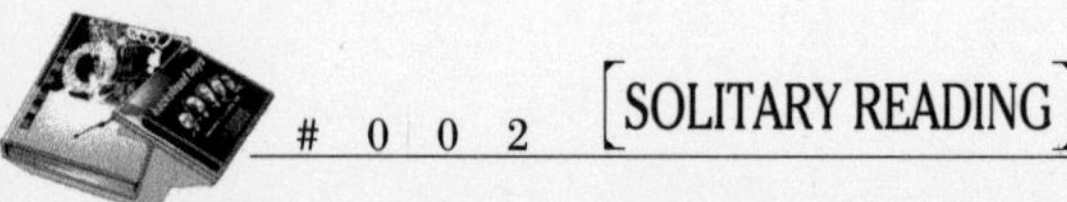

was going to go on for a while.

"You should try reading one," Kaneki said, but Hide refused.

"No, man, the books you like just go over my head. Manga's better than books anyway."

"O tempora, o mores! The youth of today, honestly . . ."

"Honestly what? You're a youth of today, too, you know! I mean, when I think about how I threw out even my favorite manga, it makes me wanna sob."

"But you didn't sob when you threw it away, did you?"

"Shut up, dude."

As they bantered back and forth, Kaneki looked back up at the TV. The news anchor was saying that this incident seemed to be the work of a Ghoul with a big appetite. *Ghouls are terrifying, even beyond what they do to their victims*, Kaneki thought.

"Takatsuki's novels make me realize that humanity is full of sin."

Hide sighed and rested his head on his hands.

When they finished hanging out at the café, they headed back to their neighborhood.

"Oh, I meant to ask, can I come over to pick up those magazines I lent you?"

"Now?"

"Yeah, I think I'm just going to go home in a bit. I'm seeing Yu later."

"Right."

Kaneki sighed. They walked to the Asaokas' house together.

"Hey, man." Once they got close to the house, Hide seemed to have something he wanted to say. "You didn't, like, try to memorize those articles in the magazines I lent you, right?"

"Uh, no? Why would . . ."

"You just seemed a little out of it this week."

A sense of relief washed over him instantly. The cause, of course, was not the magazines. *It's because my aunt is ignoring me and I'm drowning in melancholy.*

Kaneki didn't know what expression his face should have, and he looked down.

"You're so serious, man. You know, you don't have to give everything your all," Hide said, mock playfully, trying to lighten the mood. Kaneki gave a vague smile.

"You're right," he said, eventually.

"Memorization burns you out . . ."

Suddenly the mood did feel a little lighter. *Just sharing this moment, this feeling with someone else, instead of dealing with it alone . . .*

"Just wait here, I'll go get the magazines," Kaneki said, feeling embarrassed as they approached the door to the Asaokas' house. But when he opened the door, something unbelievable happened.

"Welcome home."

He'd never heard those words come out of his aunt's mouth before. He had taken off his shoes and started heading for his room when she emerged from the living room. Confused by her clearly changed attitude, he stuttered. "I just got home . . ."

"I tidied your room."

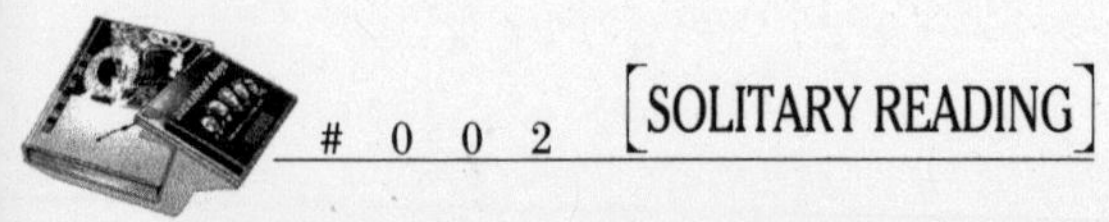

"What?"

She did not grin or say anything else. She simply returned to the living room. Although he didn't understand what she meant, Kaneki said, "All right" and went to his room.

Maybe she's changed her mind and she's trying to reach out to me now. Mom always said, if we refrain from blaming others and remain sincere, understanding will eventually come.

But he couldn't see anything that convenient happening any time soon. Still uncomprehending, he opened the door to his room and went inside.

He exclaimed in surprise.

And he froze on the spot. His bookshelf, which had been filled with all his favorite books, was now empty.

He was stunned into silence. He looked, disbelievingly, at where his books should be, but there was nothing there. Before he understood what had happened, he began to tremble. Beads of sweat formed on his forehead.

"Why?"

Kaneki moved like a shot. He felt around in the corners of the room and looked under the shelf, thinking they must be somewhere, but they were not.

He remembered what his aunt had said.

"Hey!"

He ran out of the room and rushed to the living room, where his aunt was. She looked annoyed.

"Where are my books?"

"I put them out with the recycling."

The words were like a blow to him. With each pound of his heart the terrible pain in his head grew.

"There were magazines practically bursting out of your room, you know. So I put everything together. There were so many books I had to be careful not to leave marks on the floor when I dragged the bag out of there," she said, turning back to the TV.

"But those books were important to me . . ."

"Oh, were they? I'm sorry."

No matter how pained his voice got, his aunt would not give him a second glance. It was like his voice didn't reach her. *No matter what I do, it's useless.*

Kaneki, who had to walk on eggshells just to be able to live in

this house, was in so much pain he wanted to cry.

When Kaneki came out of the house, the look on his face made Hide raise his eyebrows.

"Kaneki? What happened, man, you're pale as a ghost!"

He wiped the sweat from his brow and began to explain what had happened.

"Hide, I'm . . . I'm sorry. My aunt didn't know the magazines were yours and she threw them out . . ."

"What?"

"So I'm not sure what to do. I could buy you more, if that's all right? I mean, if they're still on sale. Are they? I'm sorry, I should've been more careful . . ."

"Hey, man . . ." Hide grabbed Kaneki by the shoulder. "Calm down! Just tell me what happened."

He bit his lip. *I can't believe this is really happening, I can't accept it. But I have to tell him.*

"My aunt put all of my books out with the recycling."

"What? All of them? What the hell?"

"Your magazines went too. I'm sorry. I'm really sorry."

"Who cares about that right now?! What happened to your books, where are they?"

What can I even do? They're not where I thought they might be. They're never coming back.

"It's too late."

If I don't tell him that I think that, Hide will go crazy with worry.

Kaneki desperately attempted to smile. Hide started to furiously run his fingers through his own hair. He turned and looked at Kaneki with passion in his eyes.

"Man, are you just going to take that?"

The feelings he had been trying to keep under control were suddenly unleashed by his friend's very serious, very un-Hide-like stare.

No, I'm not going to take it. Because those books were important to me. And the ones I bought myself were good too. But I can't lose my dad's books. They let me remember him. They eased my solitude. Why did she have to do this? What have I ever done to her? It's just too cruel—too, too cruel!

But Kaneki clamped his hands over his mouth.

In times like these his mother's voice came to him. Telling him to be a person who is hurt, rather than one who hurts others.

"It's all right."

Kaneki smiled.

"I'm fine."

As long as I live in this house, I just have to shut up and take it.

"Everything's fine."

But Kaneki rubbed his chin, as if his hand were unable to stop moving from anxiety. The gesture was reflected back to him in Hide's eyes.

"Got it," Hide said loudly, and nodded. Whether in acceptance or agreement with Kaneki's words, it was a disproportionate response. He was trying to be strong to shake off Kaneki's worries.

Before Kaneki understood what Hide meant by "Got it," Hide

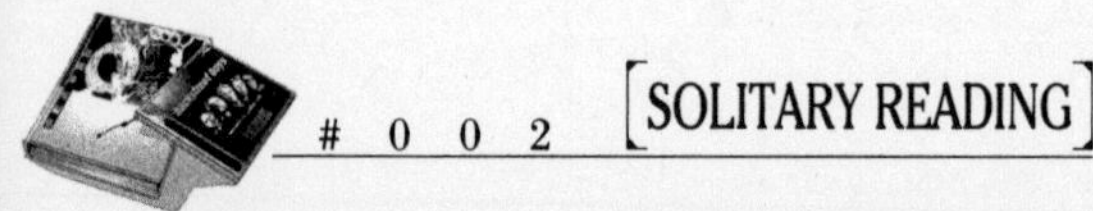

had already walked past him. He turned and saw him walking into the Asaokas' house.

"Hey! Hide!"

When he chased after him into the house, Hide was shouting. When Kaneki's aunt came out into the hallway, Hide yelled, "Did you seriously throw away his books? Some of those were mine too!"

At that, Kaneki's aunt looked upset. "Yours?"

"Yes! Really important stuff! And you actually threw it all away?!"

Hide shouted exaggeratedly, his eyes fixed on Kaneki's aunt.

"Or can I catch it before they take it all away? Oh God, and the *Yuu-chan's Sandwich Party*: 'I'll let you have some if you're good' special feature! No!"

Hide clasped his hands together like he was praying as he walked toward her. She didn't seem to want to deal with this anymore. She took a glance at Kaneki, then said, "I don't know."

"Right, I'm gonna go look! Oh, and I guess you threw Kaneki's books out by mistake, too, so I'll get those too!"

"Do as you like," she said uneasily, before grumbling her way back to the living room. Hide, full of adrenaline, pumped his fist in the air.

"All right, man, let's go!"

And just like that he ran out of the house.

"H-Hide, where are you going?"

Kaneki trailed behind him, confused by all the latest developments.

"To find your books!" he screamed.

"My books?"

"Yeah!"

Hide's facial expression all but shouted, *Well, duh*, presenting Kaneki with an option. It brought light to Kaneki's heart when he'd started to think there was nothing to do but give up.

"B-but where?"

"I told you, didn't I? How I cried when my favorite manga got thrown out?"

He told me that at the café. Not much of a story.

"Well, I studied up after that. So I know exactly where the books in this area go!"

Hide laughed confidently, then said, "C'mon, let's go!" and started off. Kaneki followed after him, his hands balled up into fists, realizing that his voice had finally reached Hide after all.

"Oh, that house. Yes, I collected them. I remember because there were so many."

When they went to the collection center and asked the staff, as soon as Kaneki said the address the trash collector knew where he meant. Kaneki and Hide turned to look at each other.

"So they are here!"

"Well, that is the thing, boys. You see, there are rather a lot of books here . . ."

It was true, there was a mountain of books behind him. Finding Kaneki's books would be like finding the proverbial needle in the haystack.

"Kaneki, will you be able to tell?"

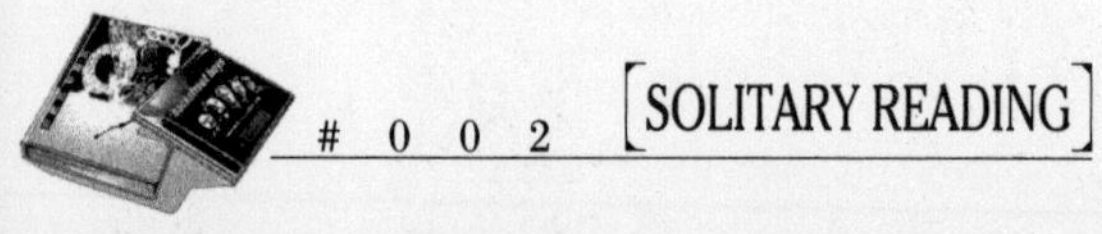

"I'll take a look."

Still, he looked hopeful that they might be there somewhere. Kaneki reached out to the mountain of books as if he were going to tackle it. Hide started looking too, for the magazines he'd lent Kaneki.

The next thing they knew, the sun had gone down and the first stars had started twinkling in the sky. Kaneki silently rolled up his sleeves and left the sweat on his brow alone—he had just found a women's magazine that looked familiar buried under some books.

"This is . . ."

He pulled it out in a hurry, only to find that it was a bundle of magazines bound together with clear tape. The cover had the name of Hide's favorite band on it.

"Hide! Magazines! The ones you lent me!"

"No way!"

Relieved that he could at least return the magazines to Hide, Kaneki held them out, but Hide didn't even look. He began digging around where Kaneki had found them.

"Look, man, your magazines . . ."

"Who the hell cares? If those were here, then your books ought to be around here too!"

He was surprised, but when he looked at where Hide was digging, he started seeing familiar covers—a bundle of books by Osamu Dazai. And that wasn't all. When he really started looking, lots of the books Hide dug out were Kaneki's.

"I've always been good at treasure hunts!" Hide said proudly.

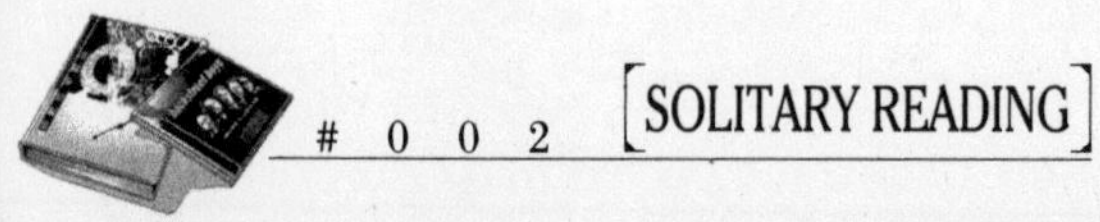

He looked ecstatic.

"Thank you," Kaneki said softly, overcome.

Hide crouched down to look Kaneki in the eye, then smiled.

"This one's soaked! That bitch!"

With that word, Hide brought it all crashing back down. Kaneki bit his lip trying to keep his face from flushing. He nodded.

"You found lots! Quite a lot indeed. Hm, shall we give you a lift back?"

The staff member looked on in sympathy at the two boys, who were exhausted from their search. He decided to send two employees with them. Once the books were loaded into a truck's bed, Kaneki and Hide got in the back too and lay down. They weren't used to working that hard, and they hurt all over, but the vibrations as they drove were a comfort to their tired bodies.

"But what if she throws them out again?" said Kaneki timidly.

"Just tell her the staff said that they were all collector's items that'll be worth something in five or six years' time! Might change her point of view if she thought there was money in it."

"But why five or six years' time?"

Hide put his arms behind his head.

"Because then we'll be adults. And when we're adults we can do whatever we want. Listen, Kaneki. Are you gonna go to college?"

"Oh, um, yeah."

"So when you go to college you can finally live on your own!"

Hide was full of good thoughts.

"On my own . . ."

"That's right! And we can hang out as much as we want! And finally have girls over!"

"Man, I don't have a girlfriend. And neither do you!"

"Idiot, I'm telling you what college life is gonna be like! All you have to do to get girls is go to college!"

"Unbelievably wrong."

But Hide's great expectations could not be stopped by a little comment like that.

"Even you might find a pretty girl who likes books!"

"W-whaaat?"

I can't keep up with Hide's positivity, but in the bottom of my heart I always thought there was a little light in the darkness. I thought I was gonna be locked away in my aunt's house forever, all freedom taken away. But I'm getting older, and soon I'll be able to stand on my own two feet.

"It's gonna be great!"

The carefree smile on Hide's face brought out a hint of a smile from Kaneki. *When I live by myself I can finally have somewhere to belong.*

"Where do you wanna live? Because I was thinking. . ." Hide asked, his train of thought still rolling ahead. Kaneki listened to him talk, as he looked up at the stars.

It wasn't long before they pulled up in front of the Asaoka house. The two staffers yelled out to Kaneki's aunt.

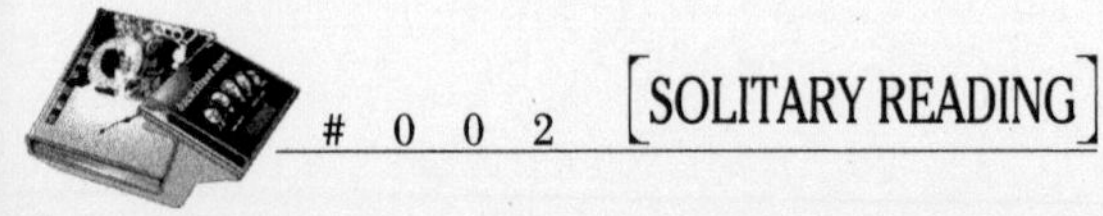

"A child who treasures books this much will grow up to be a fine man! Take good care of him."

This was uncomfortable advice for her to hear. She was not the kind of woman to listen to what others had to say. But after that, she never again interfered with Kaneki's things, perhaps thinking that anything to do with Kaneki wasn't very important at all. It was easier for Kaneki to deal with indifference, and he became a little more defiant.

Maybe this is how people actually grow up, how they change. How they become free.

Things are hard now, sure, but one day I'll escape from here.

This spark of hope became his driving force.

"Oh, Rize, your blood type's AB?! Me too!"

And then, from one cage to another—

#003 [FEMME FATALE]

The way she looks as she goes her own way, unshaken, is brilliant, and will never, ever leave me.

The Ghouls in the 11th Ward had some rules that must be strictly obeyed.

1. Don't kill on another Ghoul's hunting ground.

2. "Residence tax" was due at the end of each month.

3. One meal a month.

4. Never leave tracks.

5.

5. . .

These strict rules had been made by Hagi, the leader of the Ghouls in the 11th Ward, because the Ghouls in that area were living under the oppression of regular observation. But thanks to them, rule of order was maintained in the 11th Ward and the Ghouls there could live without fear of the CCG. They had their issues, certainly, but they never had to worry about their own safety.

Banjo Kazuichi was one of those Ghouls, nursing his resentment toward Hagi while following the rules he'd made. Other, more positively inclined Ghouls thought that, although it would be great for all Ghouls to have an equal playing field and therefore trust each other, there was no chance of it happening anytime soon.

"What are you gonna do about it anyway?" said Banjo, when suddenly, right in front of him appeared Ms. "Binge Eater" herself, Rize.

II

"Four bodies with Ghoul traces left on them have been found this month already!"

It was a meeting of Ghouls in the 11th Ward. One of the Ghouls gathered around the table, Usu, wore a pained expression across his broad face as he spoke.

"Who could it have been but you, Rize?"

The girl this line of questioning was aimed at had her nose stuck in a paperback, despite sitting in the meeting.

She lifted her gaze from the page and gave an alluring smile. She looked very calm despite currently being under fire in front of a

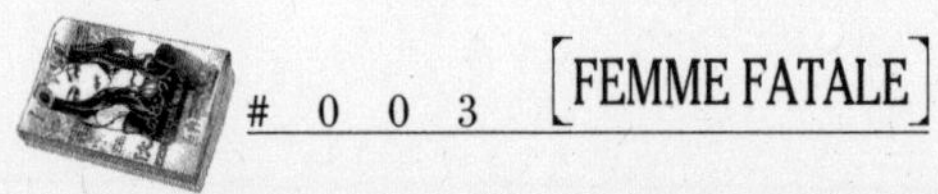

lot of people.

"Oh . . . are you talking about me?"

"Don't play dumb! This kind of thing never happened until you got here!"

Finding four abandoned corpses in one month in the orderly 11th Ward was a big deal. As Usu had said, nobody sprang to mind except Rize. The other Ghouls around the table looked at her with hard expressions too.

"The one left at the beachfront park was especially easy for people to see. Almost asking for someone to find it!"

This is a threat to our lives. And Usu is trying, through his thorough condemnation, to make her reflect so as never to do something like that again.

But then Rize tilted her head strangely. "Beachfront park?"

"Yes! A girl's body. Anything could've happened if I hadn't gone down there first thing in the morning and taken care of it!"

The 11th Ward bordered the sea, and there was a big park by the beach. *I guess Usu was the one who found the corpse.* But Rize started shaking her head in disbelief.

"I don't remember her. Maybe she was another Ghoul . . ."

"You don't even know!"

Rize looked like she was about to confess something. She did not nod.

"Usu, maybe not all of them are Rize's kills."

The Ghoul defending Rize was Yuri Akanuma, who was sitting right next to her. Yuri was a newcomer who had lived in the 11th Ward less than a year, but unlike Rize, she lived by the rules. She was attractive and sweet, blended in well with human society, had a job, and was known as a sensible person among the Ghouls of the ward.

"Then who are you saying killed them, Yuri?"

"I don't know . . . I just think pinning it all on somebody is not the right thing to do. Is it?"

Yuri looked around at the other Ghouls in the room, hoping to find someone in agreement.

"I agree. The matter should've been investigated thoroughly and confirmed before

talking about it here."

But only one person backed them up—Banjo. *Rize's the Ghoul with the street name "Binge Eater." Who else would we really think did it?* At this, Rize's eyes looked sad.

"Now, we could just as easily be talking about Hana—"

"Thank you, Banjo. But there's no help in being suspected. And they've just come here again . . ."

Banjo had tried his best to protect her, but then Hagi, who had been silent all this time, spoke up.

"She has only denied the body found on the beachfront. Rize, do you admit to the other three?"

Tension ran through the room at the sound of his voice. But Rize did not falter. "I don't know," she answered ambiguously. *She's not afraid of him. Because she knows her own strength.* She looked brilliant to Banjo.

"We will continue the investigation. But Rize, don't push your luck."

The meeting ended with Hagi's usual declaration.

"Don't forget the rules."

"It's awful to act like everything's your fault. And don't you think we should be allowed to say something when it isn't?" Yuri said to Rize, once the meeting was over and they'd left the room.

"Usu is really tough on newcomers. That was pretty rough. You All right?" Banjo said, taking the opportunity to jump in. Rize lowered her eyebrows.

"I'm not used to the system here in the 11th Ward, so there are always gonna be some misunderstandings. Thank you both for standing up for me," she said, putting her hands together in thanks. Banjo wanted to continue the conversation, but Rize seemed to want to end it there.

"If something happens again, I know I can count on you," she said, flipping her black hair, then left.

"Banjo, do you . . . like Rize?" Yuri asked him, watching Rize as she left.

"W-what? What are you talking about?"

"You're always hanging around her."

"That's—I'm just . . ."

But it was true, what Yuri said. When she was around he watched her every move, and he followed after her like he was stuck to her side. Banjo hunched his shoulders, rubbing his hands together nervously.

"Anyway, someone's leaving corpses on the beachfront. Whose work do you think it is?"

Unconcerned by seeing a big man such as Banjo fumbling like he was, Yuri continued.

"Could be another Ghoul using Rize as a scapegoat."

"What do you mean by that?" Banjo straightened his back in surprise.

"The 11th Ward is relatively peaceful because we all play by the rules, but that doesn't mean that we don't still have our Ghoul instincts. Maybe someone's been watching Rize, who still follows her instincts, and took a little inspiration . . ."

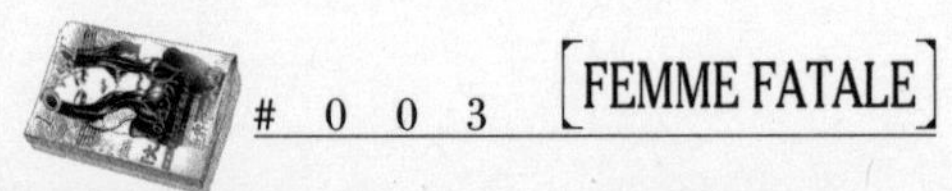

As Yuri said, Rize played by her own rules, and her instincts only seemed heightened under these oppressive conditions.

"Now anything can be pinned on Rize. Maybe somebody's just using her to piggyback off of. Poor Rize," Yuri said. Then, realizing she'd said too much, she left.

Someone's using Ms. Binge Eater as a cover. If that's true, that's unforgivable. Banjo huffed to himself.

III

"Wow, did that really happen?"

The day after the meeting, Banjo was in a room in an abandoned building used as a hangout spot, giving the full rundown to Ichimi,

Jiro, and Sante, who hadn't been at the meeting. The three of them, in matching hoods and masks, were longtime friends of Banjo's. They didn't take him very seriously because he was always unwilling to act with them.

"Well, she *is* known as the girl with the big appetite. And Usu's the one who always has to clean up. Of course he's angry," Jiro said, stating his objective opinion while flipping through a magazine.

"But there's no evidence it was her."

"Nor is there any evidence it wasn't her, Banjo," Ichimi said calmly. Banjo frowned.

"Well, Yuri has a point, you know. Right now, whatever anyone does can be pinned on Rize," Sante said, providing a voice of moderation.

"Exactly!" shouted Banjo. "I can't let someone get away with using her." He balled his hand up into a fist and looked around for agreement. Ichimi's lack of excitement was inversely proportional to Banjo's passion by a factor of one million.

"So what are you going to do about it?"

"Catch him! And if doubts become clear, then I'm sure Rize will be happy . . ."

Seeing Banjo looking so passionate, the other three were taken aback.

"Well, yes, probably."

"Might this not backfire?"

"You might get killed . . ."

"Can it, guys. Anyway, that's what I'm doing!"

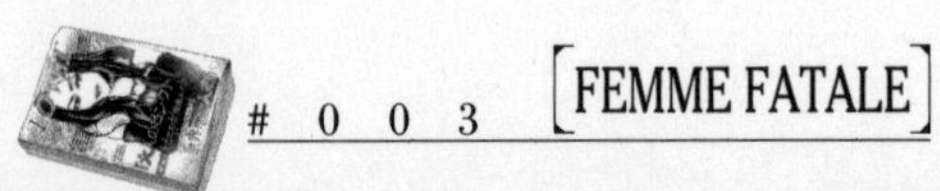

Banjo thrust his fist into the air.

"But wait, Banjo. How are you going to find the guy?"

Banjo's fist dropped weakly.

"I'll . . . I'll do my best."

"You haven't thought about this at all."

"That's very Banjo."

It was a snap decision. But I can't stop feeling like I have to do something to help her. Banjo started grappling for a solution, and the rest of them looked exasperated.

"Banjo, it's time to start gathering intelligence."

Jiro held up the magazine he was looking at to show everyone. The page he held up had a detective from a new film on it.

"Intelligence . . ."

"Usu is the one who found the body, so you should ask him first."

This genuine proposal brought Banjo back to life.

"You're right! I'd better hurry. I'll go now."

Unable to control his passion, Banjo ran off alone.

"Wait, Banjo! Do you even know where Usu is right now?" Sante yelled. It was five o'clock, the time when Ghouls started getting active in anticipation of nightfall. Usu was usually still out on patrol, nervously walking the streets from morning until night. That's why he was able to discover the bodies that Rize had left behind, but it also made him harder to find. Banjo didn't seem to have heard Sante's yell, and that worried Ichimi. He felt like he had to run after him now.

"What can we do? We gotta follow him for a while," Ichimi said, giving the instructions. He knew Banjo well. Jiro and Sante looked used to it.

"Roger that!" they said.

Banjo ran for who knows how long. *Even a Ghoul gets tired*, he thought, just as he spotted Usu.

"Usu! About that last meeting. I really don't think it was Rize's work!"

Usu frowned. "What's all this about?"

A blue vein, that symbol of frustration, popped out on Usu's broad forehead. *I guess he didn't think anyone would keep pushing it.*

"Well, the thing is . . ." Ichimi cut in. "Usu, you're the one who found the woman's body in the, uh, beachside park. What kind of state was it in? Must've been a lot of hard work, wasn't it?" He took over from Banjo and pushed for more details.

"Oh, the one on the weekend. Her stomach was slashed and all her organs had spilled out. The culprit might've taken their favorite ones and left the rest behind. I worked so hard to clean up the scraps and leave no trace. I'm hungry, too, you know, but I only have one meal a month, like we're supposed to, and then *she* comes along . . ."

Usu clicked his tongue. For those who followed the rules, Rize's actions were intolerable.

"Wait a minute, now, we don't know it was . . ."

"Hold it, Banjo. Now, Usu, are there any telltale signs that this body was one of Rize's?"

"The body at the beachfront park was more intact than the others, but they were all eaten in a thoughtless way, without concern for

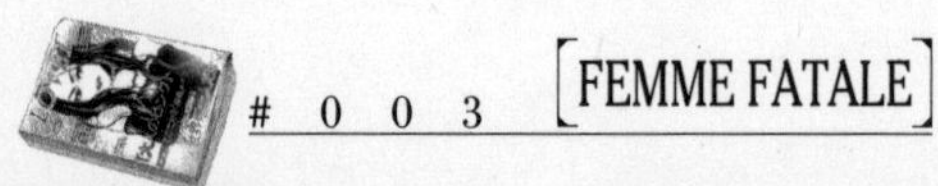

what to do with them afterwards. She messes everything up and then just leaves without a care in the world."

Rumors had been going around about the Ghoul with the big appetite for a while. Usu had been going out on patrol more than ever lately, hoping to protect his own safety more than that of the 11th Ward.

"Anyway, it's a real pain in the ass. Breaking the rules . . . How can we get free of someone like that?" Usu said in conclusion, trying to end the conversation. But Banjo slapped an arm around his shoulders.

"What?"

"Are we really free right now?"

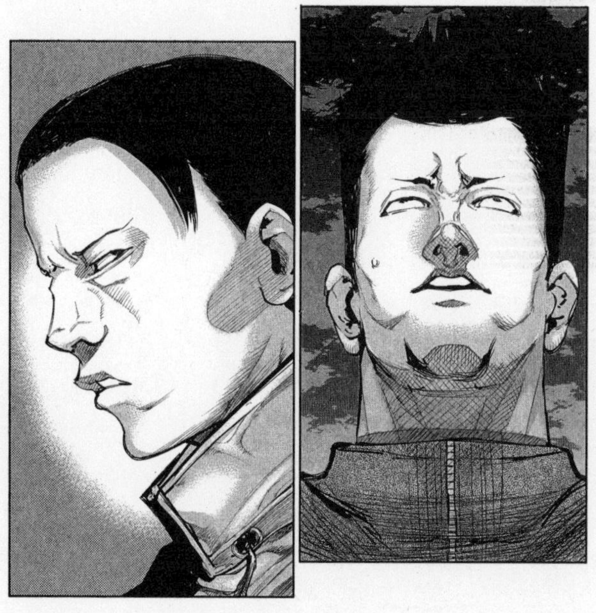

Usu furrowed his brows.

"What do you mean by that?"

"I'm so tied down by all these rules, it feels like I can't even breathe when I want. Is this really freedom?"

That feeling had come to him the day he met Rize, and it had only grown since.

"Rize can't handle that, but since everybody else sees eye to eye, who needs the rules—"

"Banjo, if you say anything else, I'll report you to Hagi," Usu said in a low voice. Banjo said nothing else.

"The way you think is selfish. There is freedom in the rules. Quit pushing your fantasies onto everyone else," Usu said clearly, then left.

"Dammit."

Once Usu was out of sight, Banjo started chewing his lip. *Pathetic of me to get scared at just hearing the leader's name. If I was stronger, I could've told him what I really think. I'm so frustrated with myself.*

"Look, Banjo, why don't we go to the beachfront park?" Jiro said, hoping to give him encouragement.

I'm so weak. I can't do much. But it's better to do something than to sit around here wasting away.

"Right! Let's go!" Banjo yelled, changing his attitude and dashing off ahead again.

The beachside park was empty at night, and the sound of the waves was all they could hear.

"I guess it's easy to attack at night."

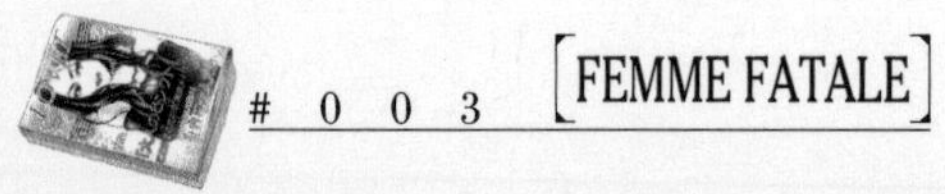

Sante sat down on a bench, looking around the park. Although they were tired from chasing after Usu, they'd all run after Banjo as fast as they could. Ichimi and Jiro took a seat too, and looked up at Banjo.

"Taking a break?"

Banjo, who was more exhausted than the three of them, sat down next to them.

"I need to know, Banjo. Do you really have this much respect for Rize?"

"Course I do. Rize has many of the things I don't have that I want for myself."

Far in the distance they could see a boat bobbing on the sea, and the lights of an industrial area farther along the coast.

"She's strong, both mentally and physically. So she can just live exactly as she wants. If I were that strong, all kinds of paths would open up to me . . . All I am is big and dumb."

As he spoke he started to feel sleepy. Ichimi saw him start nodding off and stifled a yawn of his own.

"If nothing else . . . I want to be useful to her."

It was a nice thought. But it was also what had brought Banjo this far.

"But Rize doesn't need anyone's help."

"You're right."

"I think the kindest thing to do would be to drop it."

The three of them gently trampled on Banjo's dream. "Shh," Banjo whispered, and drifted off to sleep.

IV

"Banjo, hey, Banjo!"

Even in his pleasant slumber, Banjo could hear someone calling his name. He shuddered into consciousness.

"Mmph?"

"Banjo, it's morning."

"Whoa, wait, really?"

Apparently they had all slept there on the bench together. There were women out training for marathons and elderly men walking dogs in the park. Banjo gave a great big yawn and watched them all go by happily for a moment.

"We were in the middle of trying to catch the culprit! No time for falling asleep!" Banjo said, remembering why they were there. He stood up from the bench and started to leave.

"Stop, stop! Are you looking for something?"

"Nah! I'll just investigate this park for the time being. Maybe there's some evidence."

Banjo stopped and sniffed. Usu had taken care of the body, but with blood splashed everywhere, he might still be able to pick up a scent. But no matter how hard he sniffed, all he could smell was the sea.

"No good down here. I can't smell anything."

Sante rubbed his nose.

"Dammit. I wish we'd asked where he found the body . . ."

"Definitely," Ichimi nodded in agreement.

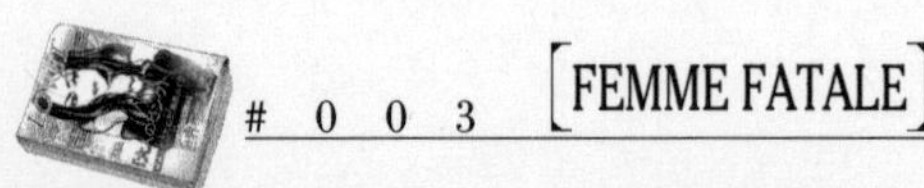

“Not much else to do but wander around the park and try to find a trace.”

“Really?”

“If I say I’m gonna do it, I’m gonna do it!”

Even if you guys don’t wanna help me, I’ll find the evidence all by myself. The others, seeing that there was no point in complaining, had little choice but to help him. The sun had just begun to rise.

“I don’t get it . . .”

In the end, all they found in the park was a baseball, a snake’s discarded skin, a lot of porno mags, and a woman’s barrette. It was the item most likely to have belonged to the victim, but it had no smell of blood to it at all. All of it was useless.

“Nice work, Usu.”

His cleanup skills had been on point as usual, but Banjo was still disappointed.

“Banjo, why don’t we go back to our hideout and come up with a strategy? The four of us hanging around in this park looks pretty suspicious.”

Ichimi was right, but it was difficult to accept that they hadn’t produced any results. Banjo looked around reluctantly at the park.

“Huh?”

Just then, he saw a young girl holding a bag, heading straight for him. She was taking fliers out of the bag and handing them out to people in the park.

“Your cooperation is greatly appreciated. We are grateful for any information. Thank you!”

Banjo stared at her intently as she came over.

"Anything you know . . . Oh."

She seemed frightened by his muscular physique, but she handed over a flier with a photo on it. "Anything you might know would be helpful," she said, nervously.

"Let's see . . . 'Mari Hirano—have you seen this girl?'"

Banjo was not great at reading, so Jiro came over and read it out for him. Sante looked at the opposite side of the flier, where the picture was. "She's really pretty!" he said.

"She's my sister," said the girl. "She was picked by a magazine as their reader model and everything."

Now that she mentions it, they do look kind of alike. She might also grow up to be a pretty girl in a few years.

"But she came to the 11th Ward last week to see a friend and nobody's heard from her since."

So she's handing out fliers trying to get some information. Banjo saw her twisting the hem of her shirt in her hands and couldn't stand to see her unhappiness, so he handed the barrette that he'd found to the girl.

"What's this?"

"Find her. Do your best and don't give up."

I guess I feel close to her because I'm also out here trying to gather information. For Rize.

"I will. I'll do my best!"

The girl clasped the barrette tightly in her hand and nodded.

"Oh, miss, what's your name?" he asked as she was leaving. She

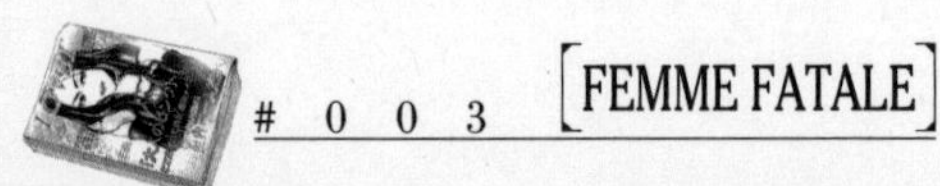

looked up at him.

"I'm Mai Hirano!"

Banjo looked straight at her. "Do your best!" he said again.

Once they'd left the girl and were on their way back to their hangout, Sante looked back at the park. "Why did you give that away? And to a human?"

"Don't worry about it. I just wanted to give her something!"

"That's just like you, Banjo. She was a pretty girl."

He looked at the photo on the flier. They all stopped to look at it again.

"Wait," Jiro said, as if he'd noticed something.

"What is it?"

"I feel like I've seen her before somewhere . . ."

"Wait, what? Where?"

With that information, the girl's troubles could all be over.

"Just a second," Jiro said and began to search his memory. But then Ichimi's face began to cloud over.

"Ichimi, what's wrong?"

Ichimi thought for a while before speaking.

"Banjo, I believe that the girl on the flier . . . is the one who was attacked by a Ghoul in that park."

"What?!"

"The girl said she disappeared last week. And Usu found that body last week."

Yes, humans are food to Ghouls. Banjo felt awful when he remembered how desperate that girl had been, but it wasn't an unlikely story.

"Before we get carried away, let's show Usu the flier."

He didn't know if Usu would still remember what the girl looked like, but it was worth a try. If nothing else, he wanted to gather more information about Rize to clear up the suspicion that surrounded her.

As they set off in search of Usu once more, Jiro yelled out in surprise.

"What, what happened?"

"I remembered! She was in that magazine!"

"What magazine?"

"The one I was looking at last night . . . the one with the feature on that detective movie." Now Banjo remembered the magazine that Jiro had been reading as he told them about the meeting.

"It's an old magazine, but I wanted to read it because it has a feature on a musician from overseas. There was a model similar to this girl in it. I'm not sure if she was a 'reader model' or not. Sorry, it's not much of a lead," he said apologetically.

"No, wait," Banjo said, folding his arms. "The more information, the better. We'd better bring that magazine with us."

They hurried off to their hideout.

"Here it is." They were at their hideout in the abandoned building. Jiro picked up the women's magazine. "Which page was it . . . I remember her because her parka was a lot like mine."

The four of them looked down at the magazine, searching for her face.

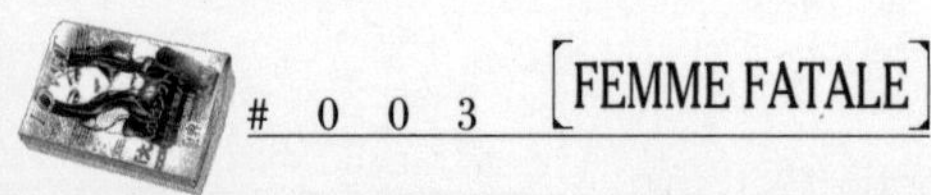

"Must be around here somewhere . . ."

"Yeah . . ."

"Who's this?"

Before they could find the girl they were looking for, their eyes latched on to another model.

"This girl . . ."

She was striking a pose and trying to look charming. And she looked a lot like Yuri, the Ghoul who had spoken up at the meeting.

Eyes wide open in surprise, Jiro pointed to the caption under the photo.

"It says her name is Yuu."

And a few pages after that, they found a picture of the girl's sister: Mari Hirano.

"Can this just be a coincidence?"

To find the two of them in the same magazine . . . Jiro looked at Banjo uneasily.

"Let's go!"

Banjo grabbed the flier and the magazine and started running toward Usu's den.

"What's wrong, has something happened?"

Usu looked up at Banjo, who was breathless from running, and gave him a disgusted look as if to say, *Not you again*. But he must've noticed something was up with them, because his voice dropped when he asked them.

"Usu, was this the girl you found in the beachside park?"

Banjo showed him the flier and magazine, and Usu's eyes

widened in surprise.

“That’s the one. I would remember a pretty girl like her.”

Banjo’s mind caught for a second, thinking about her, but the presence of Yuri on another page in the same magazine was actually more of a concern. It didn’t seem like a coincidence to him at all.

“Usu, do you know where Yuri’s house is? A woman like that must have her own house.”

Banjo wanted to go confront him directly, but what Usu said next was even more shocking.

“Yuri? What are you guys up to? She just asked me where Rize’s house was.”

The blood began to drain from Banjo’s face.

“Yuri asked you where Rize’s house is . . .”

“Yeah. She said she was moving to a different area suddenly, and she wanted to say goodbye to Rize, so she wanted to ask me where she lives . . . Hey, Banjo?”

Banjo had run off without listening to everything Usu had to say.

“Banjo! We’ve been useless everywhere we’ve gone!”

“That’s right! We’d better just leave it!”

Ichimi and Jiro tried to stop him, but he didn’t hear. *I don’t have all the answers, but what I can see doesn’t look good.* Banjo ran with all his might.

When Banjo got near Rize’s house, he saw someone and it stopped him in his tracks.

“Rize!”

She was walking alone along a bridge with few other passersby.

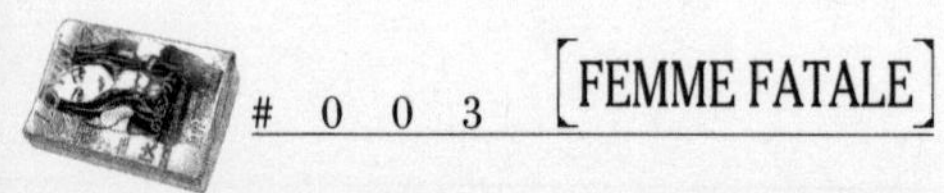

"Oh, hey, Banjo. How's it going?" she said with her usual smile, seeing how sweaty he was.

"Hey, you haven't seen Yuri, have you?"

"Yuri? Well, no . . ."

Banjo felt relieved. He tried to quickly explain everything to her.

Just then a shadow appeared behind Rize.

"Rize, watch out!"

He jumped out, arms spread to try to protect her—a moment too late. A Kagune as thick as a whip slashed into Banjo's body. The rough, scaly Kagune scraped against his skin, then struck the concrete of the bridge.

Banjo screamed.

"Are you all right, Banjo?"

Ichimi ran up to check on his wounds, but Banjo shook him off, staring at his attacker.

"You can do whatever you want, but you came here?"

Just as Banjo expected, it was Yuri standing there, her Kagune throbbing. *No doubt, she is the source of all this evil.*

"Rize! The body Usu found in the beachside park . . . She tried to pin it on you!"

"Really?"

"Yuri, you knew that girl!"

Banjo held up the flier and the magazine. He guessed that she was using Rize as cover while pretending to defend her. There certainly was enough proof of that. But then tears began to fall from Yuri's red eyes.

"She . . . Mari was my friend. We were both part-time models—that's how we met. I was with her the day she disappeared. She looked so happy when we said goodbye. But—"

Something about this isn't right. "Oh, I know what you're talking about," Rize chimed in. "Banjo, I think there's been a misunderstanding, sorry. Yuri's friend in the park?" She took a step toward him, smiling. "I'm the one who ate her. Me," she chuckled. "But all I could taste was the sea, it was awful."

"RIZEEEEE!"

Before he could say anything, Yuri launched her Kagune at Rize again. Rize blocked the attack, the Kagune bouncing off her.

Is she doing this for her dead friend? In the confusion of a situation that was nothing like they'd anticipated, Yuri screamed. "I was going to take her somewhere nice, clean her skin properly, gut her, crush her bones like sugar, then mix it up and eat her!!" Yuri's blood-red eyes suddenly drained of all color.

"W-what are you talking about?"

"Banjo, I'm not sure our presence is required here anymore . . ."

Yuri screamed as she jumped at Rize. "I'll have to eat you instead!"

Her urge to kill was like a burning flame. But Rize just smiled.

"Nice plan. Well, I offer my apologies," she said, sounding innocent and childlike. A pleasant smile came over her face.

"I'm gonna turn you into pretty little marbles!"

She absolutely refused to be attacked by anyone. And Banjo saw that now.

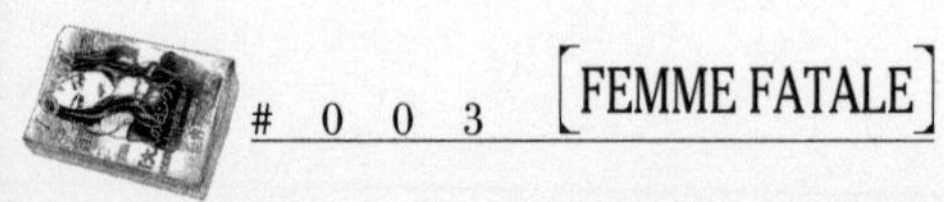

At the end of the battle, it was Yuri who was turned into pretty little marble-like blobs of flesh, which now scattered themselves to the wind.

"Is this a 'legitimate use of self-defense'?"

Rize turned and looked at him, smiling. All Banjo, Ichimi, Jiro and Sante could do was nod.

"I love to get messy but I just hate cleaning up. Probably fine if I just leave it, right?"

Without waiting for an answer, Rize started walking away. She only had one more thing to say.

"Man, I'm bored."

Yuri collapsed, now rendered into a hunk of meat.

After Rize left, Banjo realized he'd been holding his breath and coughed, putting both hands to his chest. Ichimi and the others fiddled with their masks and wiped the sweat from their brows. They were trembling after that show of tremendous power. Only Banjo felt something other than total mortal terror.

"Must be amazing to be that strong . . ."

"I'd hate it if you were like that, Banjo," said Ichimi, wryly.

"I wanna be strong . . ." Banjo said again.

Strength gives birth to violence, but there are some things that can only be won by strength. She can cut her own way with her own strength. Nothing is more beautiful than that.

His admiration did not change when news about Rize's attack got out and criticism erupted, or even when the leader and other higher-ups decided to purge her.

He remembered the very last thing she'd said as she left.

Well, take care of yourself, Mr. Leader.

Everyone else just laughed and said it was another one of her whims. But Banjo had never thought it was possible for him to be a leader. She had just been deprived of everything, but she gave that word to him freely.

"Rize put her trust in me. So I'm gonna do what I can."

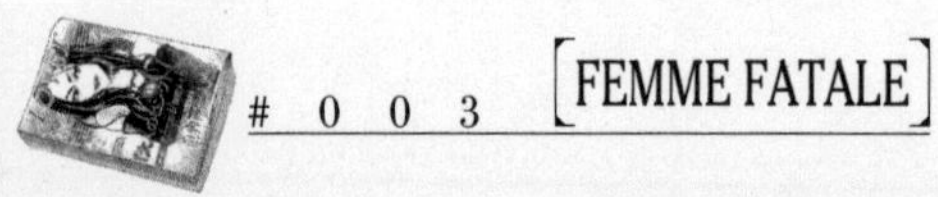

Look out for the 11th Ward. Protect those who are important.

What waited for Banjo after he broke out of his shell and took a step forward was the fate of the weak, a new kind of robbery.

#004 [INSINCERITY]

The place I stepped into, the reality I knew, the path I should've taken—my father's back.

"Now then, I'm going to announce the results of the exam the other day."

A bolt of tension ran through the Academy students as they looked at the instructor, holding the results in his hands. One student had both hands together in prayer; everyone had a sense of passion about it. The instructor looked around the auditorium slowly, then coughed.

"Top marks this time go to Mado. Of course."

It was a matter of course, and everyone in the auditorium knew it. Akira Mado, the woman of the hour, bowed to the instructor but allowed no visible change to her expression.

There is a group of monsters in this world called Ghouls that remorselessly attack and eat people. And there is the CCG, which exists to eradicate them.

And in the 5th Ward, where many educational facilities such as Teihou University are based, there is an Academy with the purpose of training future Ghoul investigators who will be the future of the CCG. They all had their different reasons for wanting to be investigators, but shared one goal, and Akira was at the top of the class in every way.

"Number one again, huh? That's just like you, Thoroughbred. Don't let it get to your head."

Seido Takizawa, one of her classmates, came sliding up next to her after the assembly to give her this warning. He was the one who always started praying when the instructor announced the results. He was the eternal runner-up, just after Akira. And his irritation showed.

Takizawa stepped into her way to block her path. Akira sighed and looked exasperated.

"That's rather arrogant of you. Let me through."

"Don't push it, Mado. It's nothing like the Academy out there on the streets."

"By the way, I saw that on this practical exam you also received an observation for . . ."

To keep him from saying anything more hurtful, Akira started talking about the minute details of Takizawa's exam results. It was clear from his expression that she was going into quite a bit more

detail than the instructor had.

"What especially stood out to me is the time delay between the release of your Quinque and its initial movement. There's a lot of time lost before you begin to attack. Your ability is still not good enough to compete with the speed of any Ghoul. You need more training," she told him in conclusion and crossed her arms. "The reason we're here, as future investigators, is to gain knowledge and experience to help us carry out our duties. Class rankings and all that is just a result of that."

"Exactly. I'm going to do great stuff when I'm an investigator, you know."

"Great. Then put the time you're using to block my way to good use and practice using your Quinque instead. Bye."

Akira unfolded her arms and walked around Takizawa. She heard him call her a bitch as she walked past, in a high-pitched, childlike whine. *I guess I got the better of him.*

But as Akira tried to make her way in a hurry, she got irritated too.

"You're amazing, Mado. Number one again."

Everybody was whispering about her as she walked down the hallway.

"Did you know her mom got associate rank when she was twenty-eight?"

"Amazing to make associate at that age as a woman. She must take after her mom."

Akira's mother—Kasuka Mado. The rumors were all

true—promoted to associate rank at age twenty-eight, then became a professor. If things had stayed as they were, she might've made it all the way to the top.

But her mother's life was cut short by a one-eyed Ghoul. This had all happened years ago now. Since then her father had raised her singlehandedly.

Her father, like her mother, was also an investigator: Kureo Mado.

"And her dad's a high-ranking investigator, too."

"Nowhere near as good as his wife or daughter, though."

They kept on whispering with no sense of shame or guilt.

Akira made it back to the dorm. She went up to her room and opened up her study materials. She was unable to get actual battle experience at the moment, but she got a feel for things when she read over case materials.

Today's was from the 20th Ward. It had few Ghoul incidents compared to other wards, and yet none of the investigators on staff there carried a Quinque. That didn't mean there weren't any Ghouls there. There were many unresolved incidents linked to a Ghoul with strange tastes they called "the Gourmet" and some unidentified Ghouls with ukaku Kagune that appeared to hunt in groups. *These creatures can only live by killing people. And the CCG is there to punish them. My father is one of them.*

Akira opened another file on her desk. This was a case that her father had been involved with. Her father's accomplishments, like the Owl Suppression Operation, did not compare unfavorably to other investigators'. *So the reason he didn't get promoted was probably me. Being in a high-rank role takes up your time, making it hard to look after children. My father must've passed up on promotions in order to raise me, a motherless girl.*

I want to figure out what happened and let everyone know my father's true strength. The thought swirled around in Akira's mind. But she didn't know where to begin.

II

Early the next morning, Akira had arrived at the Academy's training grounds early to prepare for practical training when she noticed that some others had gotten there first.

She saw Yukinori Shinohara, an Academy instructor whom she knew extremely well. Shinohara had been her father's partner for a while, and he always looked out for her.

Alongside Shinohara there were two older men. Both held attaché cases in their right hands. *Investigators. Something must've happened to make them show up at the Academy this early in the morning.*

"Oh, you're here early, Akira. Morning," Shinohara said, noticing Akira and interrupting their conversation to greet her. The two men turned to face her.

"Is she a student?"

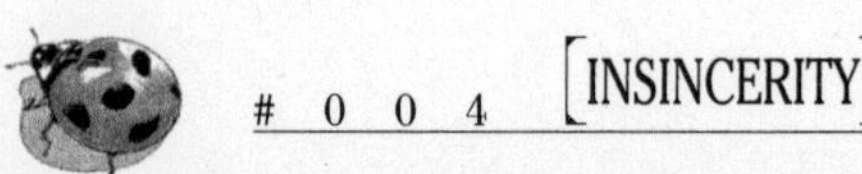

"Oh, this is Mado's kid."

It was a rather oblique comment, but the men seemed to understand instantly. One of them, a slim man who seemed to have a senior rank, narrowed his eyes as he looked at her, and she wondered what was going through his mind. But a moment later his eyes softened, searching her face.

"Wow . . . so you're Mado's daughter, the one they keep saying is top of the class this term. I'm Tada, associate rank. And this is Yanagi."

They both bowed. They were both the same age as Shinohara. A veteran unit. But Akira noticed something curious about the way Tada looked at her. *People who look at you that way are not usually your friends.*

"She's just like her mother. Thank God she's not like her Quinque maniac father."

Sure enough, now he has to go and praise my mother by saying something indelicate about my father.

"Watch it, Tada."

"What? I thought the young lady would like to hear what an excellent mother she had," he said and laughed.

Ignoring him, Akira asked Shinohara, "What happened?"

"Well, actually, last night a woman was attacked by a Ghoul in this ward. A child who lives nearby heard and yelled, so the Ghoul got away. He seems to have come in this direction."

"It's hard to imagine a Ghoul coming near the CCG Academy on purpose, but we had come to ask if anyone nearby had seen any suspicious persons, just to be certain. But it was a swing and a miss, as expected. Anyway, any Ghoul that runs at the sound of a child crying will turn up sooner or later."

Tada's prediction seemed aimed at Shinohara somehow, and Akira picked up on it.

"But if the Ghoul in question did come toward the Academy on purpose, then the Academy must hold some kind of merit to him. Can one really afford to throw away this line of investigation?"

Tada looked dazzled for a second before he began to laugh, holding his sides.

"Ha ha, what's all this now? Not even an investigator yet and she's already bossing us around! Boy, the elite sure are different after all."

"I make my judgment based on what I've heard."

"She certainly does talk a lot. Ah, youth. I was like that, too, once. . ."

After mocking her a little, Tada looked her right in the eyes.

"But if you've judged the situation incorrectly, it's your life on the line."

I probably shouldn't snap back at him. After all, I'm just a student. But Akira responded instantly, her eyes never wavering for a second.

"There's one thing I do know, though. Mr. Tada, you are too fat."

Her words had nothing to do with the previous topic of conversation. Time stopped for a moment. Akira continued, unconcerned.

"Fat is our enemy, because as humans we are always behind Ghouls in terms of speed. A second's the difference between life and

death. Taking a look at you, I'd say you have about another twenty pounds to drop. And if you don't, it's your life on the line."

Her criticism was scathing. Tada, having heard all he could take, turned bright red.

"What did you say to me?! Just because I disagreed with you, you got angry and went off like that? What, you think you can solve this case yourself?!"

In contrast to Tada's fiery anger, Akira quietly folded her arms.

"I'm just an Academy student."

"Oh, now you use that as a shield!"

"No. I'm just worried that if I solve the case, that means you're worse than an Academy student. And that, of course, would make you worse than my father, too."

"Akira, cut it out," said Shinohara, intervening. Tada stared at her.

"If you think you can do it, do it! Stupid little girl," he spat out, then left the training ground.

"Dammit, do you always have to take such a controversial stance?" Shinohara said, scratching his beard.

"What do we know about the Ghoul that ran away?"

"Hm? Oh, yeah. We have a sample of the Ghoul's saliva, found on the victim. The kid who witnessed it said the Ghoul was wearing a black mask with red spots, like a ladybug."

"A ladybug?" Comparing a Ghoul's mask to a familiar insect seemed childish to her.

"So what are you going to do, Akira?" Shinohara asked, looking tired.

"I'll need some extracurricular training," she said, not beating around the bush.

Her intuition also worked opposite from what Tada thought.

The exchange between Tada and Akira was overheard by other Academy students who came to the training ground after Akira. The story spread in an instant.

"You moron! You got into a fight with an investigator, and an associate-ranked one at that! You're supposed to listen to your elders, you know!" Takizawa said, fussing at her before their afternoon lecture.

He thinks he's got the high ground for once.

"I simply offered an opinion that he could not agree with. And

submitting blindly to what your superiors say is nothing but abdication of one's duty to think freely."

Takizawa muttered, "That's what people always say in situations like this . . ." His eyes latched on to some copies lying on her desk. "What's that? Copies from newspapers?"

"I made a copy of the article about yesterday's Ghoul attack. And all the records of Ghoul attacks in this ward in the last five years." She had spent the entire lunch break in the library.

"'Attacked and injured, but no serious wounds.' Don't you think the Ghoul who attacked this woman is long gone by now?"

"No, I don't," she said immediately.

"So what do you think?"

"I think the culprit is still near the Academy somewhere."

"But why here, with the CCG all over? It's like a mouse taking a nap next to a cat."

"That's a remarkably easy-to-understand comparison coming from you. But it's wrong."

"Remarkably, huh? All right, do you have any proof or evidence?" he said, banging his fist down on the desk. Akira raised one finger.

"Intuition."

"What?!"

Takizawa didn't know what to say, but for Akira, this was one of the most logical things to base an investigation on.

"I have faith in my intuition."

This is a battle not just against Tada, but against everyone who's put my father down.

"What do you mean?" asked Takizawa, his head spinning.

That night, Akira took all the information she had found back to her room and spread out a map. First, she put a red X where the previous night's incident took place. Then, using a color-coding system to denote cases which were thought to be linked, she put all the unresolved incidents on the map. There were lots of cases that didn't appear to have any links.

Finally, Akira marked the locations of CCG branch offices and the Academy. Then she began to see a small trend of incidents clustered around these locations.

First, the 5th Ward branch office. There was not extensive predatory behavior in the area. Ghouls have their own common sense, and apart from a few Ghouls who liked to hunt investigators, most seemed to have decided that attacking anyone in that area was too dangerous.

On the other hand, many more incidents had taken place around the Academy in the past than near any of the 5th Ward branch offices.

It didn't take a lot of deep thinking to see what that meant: it meant that the Academy was much less of a deterrent to Ghouls than any of the investigators in the 5th Ward. With fine instructors and experts at Ghoul extermination all over the 5th Ward, the Academy must look like a playground by comparison. It was natural. With that in mind, it was not too surprising that Ghouls would consider the Academy less risky to come near.

III

It was a few days after Akira and Tada's fight. Akira's classes were over for the day, so she decided to visit the staff room, where Shinohara was.

"The saliva sample found on the victim was analyzed by inspectors, but apparently it's the first time that profile has been found," he told her when she asked how the investigation was going.

"Does that mean this Ghoul has preyed before without leaving a trace?"

If there was a precedent, the CCG would have the documentation. That often offered some hints, but this time they were starting from scratch.

"This Ghoul has been very careful."

Tada had talked loudly about how any Ghoul who was scared off by a child would be found sooner or later, but the investigation seemed to have hit an unexpected wall.

"Tada's going to start investigating around the Academy today."

Now that the information available was limited, he was taking even negative comments.

"His prospects aren't bad as an associate."

"Hm. Well, Tada hasn't been very well lately."

Shinohara furrowed his brows, looking worried.

"Although your technique improves with experience, as you get older your body slows down and your mind doesn't work as fast as it did when you were younger. It's a constant battle at our age."

Shinohara also muttered something about this case being the particular battle that Tada had chosen to fight.

"He ought to lose some weight first."

"Ha ha, well, I think so too. But Tada's the kind of guy who's always looked like that and has racked up successes in the organization anyway. He's not like you; in fact, he may be your polar opposite. But he's always respected your mother."

That's nice, but it doesn't make me any less unhappy about the way he talked about my father. That's why I want to solve the case first and find this Ghoul. The ladybug. Where can it be?

Suddenly something worried her.

"How old was the child who saw the Ladybug?"

"Oh, about five or six."

"And a child that small

screamed so loud that a Ghoul ran away?"

Shinohara laughed. "Oh, right. He didn't just scream, he yelled, 'Mr. Inspector, come right away!' A very quick-witted child."

Now she understood why the Ghoul had escaped. Akira thanked Shinohara and left the staff room. But as she walked down the hallway she suddenly stopped.

Could such a young child really think so quickly on their feet to scare off a Ghoul this good at covering their tracks?

It was a casual question. But once she'd asked it, the scope of the question expanded. Perhaps it was a clue. Akira quickly left the Academy as if she were being pulled somewhere.

Is that the kid?

Akira had headed straight for the scene of the crime, on the outskirts of the 5th Ward. A boy was kicking a pebble on his own in a little alley near a row of houses—the kind of boy you would see anywhere, but this kid seemed strangely gloomy.

"Are you Shota?" she called out, using the name she'd found out earlier. The boy looked up.

"Who're you?"

"I'm Akira Mado. A future Ghoul investigator."

"Future investigator?"

"You can call me Akira. I wanted to ask you some questions about what happened the other day."

The boy looked down and kicked another stone.

"My grandma and granddad are already angry at me about what a dangerous thing I did. I don't wanna talk about Ghouls anymore."

His grandparents had every right to be angry, since if something had gone wrong the boy would be dead now.

But she decided to ignore their feelings and asked him, "So your grandparents would prefer it if that woman had died?"

"It's not like that," the boy began. "My mom and dad were both killed by Ghouls."

He kicked a stone toward the wall. It bounced off and disappeared somewhere.

"What do you want to know?" She heard the darkness in his heart that would not go away, the pain of having his parents taken away. Akira herself knew that feeling.

"How did you realize there was a Ghoul?"

"It was night, I looked outside for some reason, and I saw a woman walking past the house. Then, behind her, a man."

"How did you know he was a Ghoul?"

The boy looked up at her silently. Akira looked back at him, seeing him now as another human being, not just as a child.

"It was the guy who took my dad away."

Akira didn't know what to say. The boy clenched his fists.

"A little after my mom was killed by a Ghoul, my dad and I were attacked by some other Ghouls. He told me to run away, so they only got him. So I knew that Ghoul when I saw him. I'd know him anywhere."

The tangled thread of the case was starting to unravel.

"When did that happen?"

"It was when I was in kindergarten. We lived in the 20th Ward.

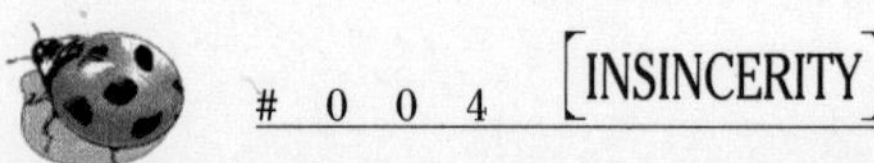

When they finally found my dad, there was another body there too. All torn up. It was a Ghoul. They said he was killed by another Ghoul after he killed my dad."

If he's in elementary school now, then this must've happened last year or the year before. Akira tried to remember the cases in the 20th Ward that she had looked at the other day. Among them, there had been a report about a mysterious group of Ghouls with ukaku Kagune that hunted together. A group of Ghouls from an organization called Futamaru had been killed by an ukaku in the 20th Ward.

"I thought the guys who killed my dad were all dead, but this one wasn't. I thought he was going to kill the woman who walked by my house, so I chased after them."

As she listened to his story, Akira realized there were so many new possibilities. If it was a Ghoul who belonged to Futamaru, he may have fled here from the 20th Ward after losing the battle against the Ukaku Ghouls. And still in fear of the Ghouls who killed his friends, he would've been looking for a safe place to hunker down. *And this is a safe place.*

Standing on the shoulders of giants. Most Ghouls wouldn't come near the CCG at all. Everyone kept saying that after he was spotted by the boy the Ghoul had fled to the Academy, but couldn't he have also fled *back* to the Academy? The idea stuck in Akira's mind.

It was possible that he always stayed near the Academy and kept a watchful eye over it. That meant he would know that there were investigators after him. This cautious Ghoul had taken note of Tada and the others and run away.

Perhaps this is all I can do as an Academy student. From here, Shinohara and the 5th Ward branch office investigators would have no choice but to investigate the Academy and its surroundings. But it was also possible that they'd need clearer evidence to start investigating. Still, they had to act now.

"Thank you for your cooperation. See you," Akira said, thanking the boy. She started to leave.

"Akira," he said, calling her name. "Did you lose somebody to a Ghoul too?"

She turned around. The boy was looking straight at her. She had noticed something gloomy about him; had he noticed the same thing about her?

"My mom," she answered frankly.

"Oh," he said. "Is it still tough? Am I gonna be all right when I'm a grown-up?"

"I don't know . . . it's different for everybody."

"But are you? Are you okay now?"

He can't see the light at the end of the tunnel right now.

"I'm—" Suddenly an image of her mother crossed her mind, then her father. And when their images combined, she saw herself reflected back at her. "It's a secret," she whispered.

"Right," laughed the boy. Suddenly there was a glint in his eyes.

"My dad told me before he died that I should forget all about Ghouls. And my grandma and grandpa tell me I shouldn't take any risks. But . . ."

He lifted his right arm and pointed straight ahead, in the

direction of the Academy.

"The day after, I went the way that the Ghoul ran. And I found them there."

Akira's eyes widened in surprise.

"They didn't have their masks on, but I knew it was them. I followed them and found where they live. Akira . . ."

There was a fire in his eyes now.

"Akira, please . . . find the guys that killed my dad . . . and kill them!"

Anger, sadness, and resentment. And this young child has to bear them all. Another Ghoul tragedy.

The sun was setting, and a cool wind blew through. A man struggling under lots of bags appeared from the run-down apartment building, where many students lived. He was in his early to mid-twenties. He

went down the rusty stairs, then looked around, setting his gaze far into the distance. Toward the Academy.

"I'll come back when things have cooled down."

He smiled to himself and started walking toward the Academy. To escape from the net of the investigation that was tightening around him.

"Unfortunately, that's not gonna happen."

A woman's voice echoed behind him.

He turned around and saw her standing in the middle of the street. Akira's glossy hair swirled around her in the evening breeze as she stared him down.

"Former Futamaru executive . . ." Her words visibly affected him. But he quickly smiled and dropped the bag he was carrying to the ground.

"You're wearing an Academy uniform. You must be a student. I don't know what you're here for, are you sure you've got the right man?"

He rummaged in his bag, then pulled something out.

"It's been an unlucky couple of days. You've seen my face, so now you have to die!"

He had pulled out his mask, a black one with red dots that the boy had described as being like a ladybug. The man—the Ghoul—closed the distance between them almost instantly.

Akira stumbled back in surprise, but he swung at her and his fist grazed her cheek.

"Aren't you vain?!" he shouted, angry at the way she'd deftly

dodged his attack. He created a little distance, crouching down on the ground, ready to pounce.

"But hey . . . 'like a moth to the flame!' " As he spoke his flesh and clothes ripped and a reddish-black fog was released. It immediately coalesced and transformed into a thick, undulating Kagune—a bikaku Kagune.

"What are you gonna do, you poor baby? You don't even have a Quinque!" he cackled.

"But I do," she whispered. He didn't hear her. His Kagune began

to stretch. "Let me introduce it to you."

There was darkness in Akira's eyes.

"My Quinque is my father."

The small, sharp-pointed bullet shone like a chestnut.

The Ghoul screeched.

Akira got down on the ground as the bullet pierced the Ghoul's body.

"When you said she was like a moth to the flame . . . well, I think you're more perceptive about yourself, really."

Kureo Mado stepped out, holding Rai, an ukaku Quinque from his collection, in his hand.

"When it comes to insects, the best thing is to burn them out!"

Right after she saw the boy, Akira called her father. Fortunately, he had just finished work and said goodbye to his partner, so he came as Akira's 'Quinque.' And his Quinque had shown its overwhelming power to Akira.

The Ghoul, pounded into the ground by Kureo's attack, begged and pleaded for his life, but it was absolutely meaningless. And as proof of that, Kureo laughed.

"When we heard you guys lost to the Ukaku Ghouls, we got you a little something. A little present. Do you want it?" Kureo walked up to the Ghoul, his Quinque in front of him. "It's a present of horror!"

He activated the Quinque at close range. Small bullets blasted through the Ghoul's mask, eyes, nose, mouth, and brain. The destroyed mask fell to Akira's feet with a clang.

It was more black than I realized, Akira thought, and then realized something else. *The name Futamaru can also mean "twenty." The mask was supposed to be a twenty-eight-spotted ladybug.*

"What's all this about?"

Tada, who had been investigating in the area, came running up. He had been hot on the Ghoul's trail too.

"Good to see you, Tada. I hear you've been looking after my daughter recently."

"Mado! What are you doing here?"

Tada was first surprised by Mado, then by seeing Akira at his side, and then finally by the Ghoul who lay writhing on the ground.

"Is this the guy?"

"Akira figured out his whereabouts."

Tada looked at her in disbelief. She gave him a smile.

"We retrieved the Ghoul's Kagune, too. I was thinking about turning it into a Quinque in your honor, Tada."

Tada's lips began to tremble. "Like father, like daughter!" he spat.

Is that supposed to be an insult? Akira smiled again.

"That is the highest praise," she said.

IV

A few days later she went to tell the boy that the Ghoul had been destroyed. "Right," he said, fiddling with a stone. Happiness was not the right emotion for the occasion. Killing these hated enemies wouldn't bring back his dead parents.

"Without what you told me, that Ghoul would have gotten away again. And there would have been more victims. You didn't just save one woman's life. As long as Ghouls exist, they'll keep killing."

Akira finished filling him in, then turned around to leave. When she was a fair distance away, the boy called out her name. She turned around and saw him struggling to say something.

"Thank you," he said finally.

She left and headed back to the Academy. When she got there, she saw someone near the entrance.

Is that my dad?

It was. Her father waved to her.

"Why are you here now?"

"I left work early. I have two things to tell you."

"Go on."

"First. Tada's on a diet now." Instead of losing all confidence after being trashed by a student at the Academy, he had actually found inspiration in it. *That stubbornness is probably why he's still here.*

I learned a lot from this case. I beat Tada, but I didn't do it alone. I feel bad about admitting that Tada is right, but he's right—I am *young, I don't even have a Quinque. What I have to do now is work hard to become an investigator who can stand on her own. A bit of teething.*

"Second. I found a curry place that's perfect for eating on the go, but my partner's not into spicy food. He has no clue how good curry is. Wanna go?"

Her father's words cheered her right up. She looked at her watch and nodded.

"Perfect time for a meal."

Someday I want to be the one who helps my father. I want to protect him, like he protected me, she thought as she walked by his side.

But Akira's father would never get to see her grow up to be an investigator who could stand on her own two feet.

Her father's life would be taken by a Ghoul called "the Rabbit." Akira would never forget how his body had been torn to shreds. Still, she carried her father's love with her wherever she went.

I want to protect the man my father respected so much, whatever happens.

She was on her way to meet him.

The man who overcame loneliness to walk his own path, the man who respected my father with all of his heart.

My father's last partner, my first partner—Kotaro Amon.

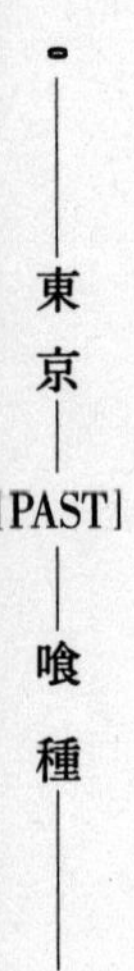
TOKYO
東京
[PAST]
喰種
GHOUL

#005 [MATCHING]

It doesn't matter what you are.

"Hey, we're talking about going somewhere for the three-day weekend, you wanna come?"

I had just gotten used to living alone in Tokyo when my mother called to ask me this.

"On a trip?"

"Yes. Now, I know it might be difficult what with school and all, but I thought it couldn't hurt to ask."

Kimi Nishino. *My parents put a lot of thought into my name, but it's just plain. But with my diligence and commitment to my studies, now I'm a medical student at Kamii University in Tokyo.*

"This upcoming three-day weekend . . . it might be tough, I have a paper to write," Kimi said, looking at the schedule book in her hand. She was still in her first year, which meant that she hadn't finished the classes she needed to take the national admissions test, because they lasted all year, but she had been accepted to the college. And since she'd signed up for enough classes to make your eyes water, she had a lot of papers to write. Even in her spare time she studied—her desire to be a doctor was that strong.

"Just as I suspected. I understand. We'll bring you back something—you just keep at your studies."

"I will. Sorry, mom. Tell everyone hi for me."

I wonder if she really did anticipate that I'd say that. Both said, "Bye now," at the same time and hung up.

"A trip . . ."

Kimi set her phone down on her desk and stretched. Now that she thought about it, her younger brother wasn't planning to take college entrance exams next year. *Everyone's going traveling while they still can. Maybe I should go.*

But I'll have another chance someday.

Kimi returned to her paper.

"Morning, Kimi. Did you finish that paper?"

"She's not like you, you know. Of course she did."

The next day, when she went to the campus, some of the girls in her department called out to her. First was Shiraishi, a smiley girl who was always in full makeup. Next to her was Itose, a doctor's daughter.

"Yeah, I finished it," Kimi said, sitting down next to them.

"All you do is study, Kimi. Don't you ever wanna hang out with

us?" Shiraishi said, her eyes twinkling.

"Don't listen to her, Kimi. She's just trying to find someone to go on a blind group date with us."

"Hey! Everybody's really excited about it, and we don't have enough people!"

Shiraishi looked like she'd been caught. *Every time I see her she does this.*

"But you don't have a boyfriend, do you, Kimi? Nobody to hang out with, no smart and sexy college man . . . What are you doing for the three-day weekend? A boyfriend is a must-have for any college girl!"

I don't have a boyfriend and I turned down a trip with my family. And I can't imagine I'll find someone on a group date, as plain a woman as I am.

"I'm sorry, I'm busy that day."

"What? What are you doing?"

"Quit hounding her. God, you're annoying," said Itose.

"What about you, Itose? You wanna come?" Shiraishi said, changing tack. Her hands were clasped together.

"My sister's bringing her fiancé, so I'm going to hang out with them."

Itose's sister was a nurse working in a university hospital, and her fiancé was apparently a doctor from work.

"Wow, is that what it's like in a doctor's family? I wanna man like that. . ."

"Then you should work on developing some character. . ."

"Don't talk to me like that! I have tons of character! I'm full of it!"

"Just look up 'character' in the dictionary."

Itose was seriously amused by Shiraishi as she scrambled to respond. Their exchange sounded like a comedy routine, and Kimi couldn't help but laugh.

"Enough," Shiraishi said, puffing out her cheeks exaggeratedly, and Itose started laughing too.

When their morning lecture was over, the three parted ways. Kimi bought her favorite pastry at the campus bakery and sat down on a bench outside. Kamii was a giant college with a big campus and lots of greenery. The soft light falling through the leaves of the trees was soothing to the eye.

College life is good. The only thing I don't have is a boyfriend, like Shiraishi said.

Kimi had only had one boyfriend ever. When she was a freshman

in high school, an older boy had told her how he felt and they had gone out. But the first date didn't go so well, and things naturally fizzled out. And then nothing after that.

But she was satisfied with how things were now. She was getting closer to her classmates, and day by day she was getting used to living in the 20th Ward. It was full of excitement she couldn't have found back home.

She took a big bite of her pastry and muttered, "So good," to herself, her cheeks puffed out like a hamster. *Couldn't have found this back home either.*

Just another normal day as a normal person. She imagined it would always be like this.

Until the moment when it all suddenly came to an end.

II

It was the first day of the three-day weekend. After staying up late working on her paper, Kimi didn't wake up until the sun was already high in the sky. She checked the time on her phone. One o'clock.

She had an email from her brother. The subject was "Pictures," and when she opened it she saw that he had attached tons of photos from their destination.

"Nice..."

A lush green lawn. Her mother, who wasn't very good with technology, must have asked her brother to send the pictures to her.

"Thanks. Wish I was there," Kimi replied to her brother. He replied right away.

"Wish you could've made the time to come."

It seemed like he wasn't having a good time on the trip with his parents. But the trip had just begun. They were still in the car.

"Tell dad to drive carefully," she wrote.

"He says 'gotcha,'" her brother wrote back, bringing the conversation to an end. Kimi got out of bed, fixed herself something to eat, and turned on the TV.

The first item on the news was about Ghouls. Some Ghouls had appeared in the 5th Ward and were trying to attack people.

Fortunately, a little kid had gotten suspicious and reported a Ghoul to the CCG, who caught him right away. They showed the boy, who had himself been attacked by a Ghoul before, and had managed to save a woman's life this time. It was captioned "Elementary school student, hero." The boy said, "I want to work at the CCG when I grow up."

"Ghouls, yeesh . . ."

The 20th Ward was not as dangerous as some of the other wards, but it was still a concern for women living on their own, like Kimi. There were many things nobody knew about Ghouls, and many rumors about them too. Kimi wondered what they were like. *Of course, they're terrifying, and I don't ever want to meet one, but I feel like there are things you can't know about them unless you see them.*

After that, she watched a talk show for a bit, then turned off the TV when she got tired of it. She took her dirty dishes to the sink and washed them, humming to herself. She had only a very loose plan for the day, and she was thinking about going to a restaurant she'd heard was nice when her phone rang.

"Coming!"

She dried off her hands and ran to her phone. It was one of her relatives, who lived in the same neighborhood as her parents.

"That's odd," she thought and answered the phone. What she heard ended all illusions of this being a normal day.

"Kimi! Are you there? Your family's been in a car accident!"

Suddenly the ground shook and twisted beneath her.

They had been going down a narrow road with lots of sharp turns when they had a head-on collision with an oncoming car, and they had been transported to the emergency room.

That was all she knew. Without much more to go on, she went to an ATM and got out all the money she could, then hopped into a taxi. It would take at least two hours to get there, no matter how fast they went. Her heart was pounding in her chest and she couldn't breathe. She felt dizzy.

She tried calling her family's phones over and over again. She just wanted to hear their voices. But they didn't answer, and her phone was starting to die. She looked again at the text conversation she'd had with her brother that morning. Everything had been normal then. Her fingers trembled with worry as she tapped out a message to him: "Where are you? Are you all right?"

"Please be all right..." She hoped and prayed, but no response came.

By the time she got to the hospital, the sun had already started to set. She jumped out of the car and ran into the hospital.

"Excuse me! My name is Nishino, Kimi Nishino! My family was in an accident..."

"Just a moment, please," said the receptionist. Soon, someone who appeared to be a doctor arrived.

"Where are they? My mom, dad and brother?"

The doctor looked at her, a pained expression on her face.

"Why are you looking at me like that?"

"Your parents died instantly. Your brother died on the way here..."

"What... what do you mean?"

He showed her to the morgue. When he opened the door, the cold air made the hair on her arms stand on end. There were three bodies lined up. *I knew this was coming, but I wasn't ready.*

"This is your family, correct?"

The doctor's words made her want to run away. The distance between her and the table was not far, but she felt like she was walking through mud to get there. *It can't be true, it can't be true.* She reached out and touched the first body, gently lifting the sheet to reveal her father's face. He was covered in bandages. Kimi's face crumpled.

Trying desperately not to collapse to the ground, she reached for the next sheet. Her mother's face was far more damaged than her

father's. Kimi's head ached, and she couldn't think. Her knees began to shake. Now she stood in front of her brother's body. She reached for the white sheet.

"It can't be."

There was her younger brother, wounded but looking as if he were asleep.

"It can't be!"

Kimi grabbed her brother's shoulder and started shaking it. She screamed again, trying to wake him. She screamed until her throat was sore. But he did not wake up.

Everyone. My mom, my dad, and my brother. My whole family.

"I want to wake up now!" she screamed.

All gone in an instant.

Her memory was vague after that. She spoke with the police and got her relatives to

come, and then the wake and the funeral passed. The truck driver who had crashed into them had also died. Since everyone had died in the accident and there were few witnesses, it was difficult to determine the cause of the accident, but the police seemed to think both parties had been negligent.

A week after the funeral, Kimi returned to her apartment in the 20th Ward. Her relatives had told her to take a break from school for a while, but she couldn't. "I have to go back to classes," she said.

I told my mom when she asked me to go on the trip with them, 'It might be tough, I have a paper to write.' And what did my mom say? 'You just keep at your studies.'

"I'm gonna be late for class. . . I gotta get to campus. . . Gotta write this paper. . ."

Kimi paced around her room, then spread her textbooks out on the table.

"What do I need to do? What should I be doing?"

But she couldn't think. Every time she tried, her head began to hurt. She put her hands to her forehead and sat down.

But her eyes darted around the room, looking for her phone, not another textbook. She picked it up and opened her messages. She had read her brother's messages so many times she had them memorized. And the picture of that magnificent scenery.

I bet they were smiling when they looked at that view. Saying they wished I was there.

Kimi felt hot and dizzy suddenly. And she just kept feeling hotter.

She heard her mother asking her if she wanted to go on a trip.

Her brother sending her a picture because she couldn't be there.

Her father, whose response to being asked to drive carefully was, "Gotcha."

And she would never see their faces again.

She covered her face with her hands. She couldn't stop her tears from falling.

"I can't . . . I can't take it."

They died. And they left me behind.

III

On her first day back at classes, she walked into the auditorium and saw Shiraishi and Itose. Shiraishi sounded as happy as ever, but today all she said was a very proper, "Good morning."

"I saw what happened on TV. It's terrible . . ." Itose said.

"Thanks," said Kimi. It was all she could do to say it. Neither of the girls said anything else.

It had been a while since she'd been to class. She desperately tried to follow the professor's words, or keep up with what he wrote on the blackboard. But nothing stuck in her mind.

Oh no, she muttered to herself when she looked down at her blank notebook page at the end of class.

Eventually she realized that she wasn't going to be any good that day, and went home. On her way home, as she walked toward her house, she kept bumping into one person after another. And when she got home, she thought about her family and started to cry again. She couldn't sleep that night, and before she realized it, it was morning again. Time for class.

She had no appetite but knew she had to have something in her system, so she forced herself to drink something and eat some gelatin, but nothing had any flavor to her. Not even her favorite pastry appealed to her anymore.

Her notebook was still blank. And time was passing quickly without her writing anything down. *I can't remember how I made it through life all this time.*

Am I losing it?

She sat down on a bench on campus, a can of orange juice in her hand, and wondered about her own sanity. Even the light coming through the leaves of the trees hurt her eyes now.

Everyone in her department knew, and they were all giving her some distance. Her friends from home just watched because they didn't know what to say.

She was alone in the world.

"I wish I'd gone with you . . ." Nobody could hear her, but Kimi whispered it out loud anyway. "I wish I'd gone with you . . ."

I wish I'd died with you . . .

Do I even need to come to classes anymore? Doctors save people's lives, but I've already lost the people most important to me. So there's nothing left for me to learn here.

I'm already dead anyway.

The moment I lost my family, my heart was torn apart and I died. All that's left is an empty shell.

I want to see my dad. And my mom. And my brother. I want to see them all. It was the only thing she wanted, and her desire grew stronger by the second.

The can of orange juice, barely touched, fell out of her hand and hit the ground. The juice gushed out, going everywhere, and the mouth of the can was covered in dirt and grass.

Kimi picked up the empty can and sighed.

"I gotta pull myself together."

She stood up from the bench and walked over to the vending machine to throw the can away. She put some coins in the machine and bought another juice. The can was dispensed with a thud. Kimi picked it up and headed off to her next lecture. She was annoyed as she climbed the stairs to the auditorium.

Somewhere in the distance she heard other students having fun. *And I'm stuck here alone, feeling like I want to disappear.*

"Hey," someone said behind her. Surprised, she turned around reflexively and saw a man coming up the stairs behind her. He was slim and tall with glasses and a nice smile. *Is he in my year?*

"You forgot your change. In the vending machine," he said, and showed her the change in his hand. *I guess I forgot it when I bought the juice. And he brought it to me.*

"Th-thank you," she stuttered and took the change. Normally, the conversation would've ended here. But the boy had other ideas.

"Are you a freshman? What's your name?"

Confused, she said, "Nishino."

"Nishino? I'm Nishiki!" he laughed.

The only people who had talked to Kimi lately were people who knew that she had lost her family. She'd looked at so many concerned, caring, slightly troubled faces that his smile was utterly dazzling to her. She looked away, feeling slightly uncomfortable. *I don't want him to see me look upset.*

He was so kind to bring me my change. But I don't know how to be around people right now. I don't want to bring him down.

But what he said next surprised her. "Ms. Nishino, can I have your phone number?"

"What?"

The word fell out of her mouth immediately.

"Let's go out sometime."

"Huh?"

Although she kept speaking nonsense, his eyes stayed fixed on her. Maybe he didn't mean anything by it, but Kimi couldn't understand why someone this attractive would want to go out with her.

"What's your number?"

He got out his phone and took down her number. She still didn't understand what was going on, but she got out her phone too.

"Nishiki, right?" she said as she entered his name.

He grinned in confirmation.

"Nishiki Nishio, but everyone calls me Nishiki."

"All right, Nishiki."

"I might be in touch tonight," he said, waving as he left. Kimi

was left standing there on her own, stuck to the spot. She wondered if she'd been daydreaming, but when she checked her contacts, she saw his number there and knew that it had really happened.

And that was how she met Nishiki.

That night when she got home, she set her phone on the table and stared at it.

"Maybe it was just a joke."

Of course it was. What could a guy like that, who knew how to talk to women, want with a girl like her?

But just that little spark of something happening had reminded Kimi what real life was like. That she had once spoken to people like that on a daily basis.

But it didn't take long for that spark to fade. She remembered her family again and threw herself down on top of her desk. Sadness welled up within her. *I wish I could fall asleep and never wake up. I wish tomorrow would never come.*

Suddenly she heard her phone buzz with a new message. She grabbed it to check and saw NISHIKI.

He really did *get in touch.* Still surprised, she opened the message.

"Hey. What are you up to?"

She looked at her textbooks. "I'm studying," she wrote. An informative reply. Nervously, she hit send.

"Impressive," he wrote. "By the way, what's your major?"

"Medicine," Kimi wrote. Soon enough another reply came from Nishiki.

"Amazing. I'm in pharma studies. Maybe we have some classes in common?"

That's how their freewheeling, anything-goes conversation started. There was no pity or compassion in his words. He didn't know anything about her loss, which was why Kimi could talk to him. Part of her was so relieved.

"We should study together tomorrow," she wrote, finishing the conversation for the evening. "Night."

*I know it was all by text, but that's the first time in a long time that I've had a real conversation. S*he felt exhausted all of a sudden, now that the tension of their conversation was broken. She was tired, yes, but she was also sleepy. Kimi rubbed her eyes and got into bed.

And she slept like a log.

IV

The next day, she was surprised when she woke to find her room flooded with sunlight.

"How long did I sleep?!"

She had an early class that day, but there was no way she was going to make it. She needed to start getting ready for her other classes, but she simply stood in front of her sink staring at her face in the mirror. She had slept solidly, but the accumulated exhaustion still showed on her face.

"Why did he talk to me?" Kimi muttered, pressing her hands to her pale cheeks. She finished her morning routine and left her house right on time.

"You came!"

"H-hello . . ."

When her lectures were over she went to the place where they'd agreed the previous night to meet. Nishiki was already there. She had only half-believed that he would show up, so when she saw him standing there waiting for her she looked at him incredulously.

"What's up?"

"Oh, um, nothing," she said, averting her eyes so as not to be rude.

"Ooh, you're stubborn," Nishiki said, and laughed. "You don't have to be so polite, you know. What's your first name again, is it Kimi? Can I call you Kimi?"

"Y-yes, you may."

"Again with the formality." Nishiki smiled.

"There's a table over there," she gestured.

They walked over to the table on the sunny terrace and sat down facing each other across the table. Nishiki took his books and supplies out of his bag. Kimi's eyes widened. He didn't seem like a serious person, but his books looked well-used.

"If I try to study alone I just blow it off, so watch me, all right?" he said, and started studying.

Kimi hurriedly got her books out too. She wasn't sure what to study, but then she remembered all the gaps she had to fill in since

the day of the accident, and she got to work.

While they were studying, Nishiki did not speak enough to disrupt them. *I feel nervous every time he speaks, but I'm not uncomfortable.*

They studied until the sun set and only said goodbye after making more plans.

"Why me?" The question wouldn't go away. But part of her was starting to feel better.

They kept making plans to study. Eventually they started making plans to hang out. They spent more and more time together.

Nishiki had gotten a little more casual since they'd met. And Kimi could talk to him now without any hesitation.

Now she could hardly wait for tomorrow, when not that long ago she had wished it would never come again. When she was with Nishiki, her pain didn't seem that bad anymore.

"I heard Kimi's going out with Nishiki Nishio."

She overheard someone gossiping about her as she sat on a bench on campus, waiting for Nishiki to come. She looked and saw Shiraishi and Itose walking side by side. Being the topic of conversation made Kimi feel awkward, so she hid behind a nearby tree. They took no notice and continued talking.

"Someone saw them together at a festival wearing kimonos. Everyone's gossiping about them being a couple, but isn't it obvious? Nishio doesn't have the best reputation when it comes to relationships, so how true can it be?"

"Nishio's so hot, how is he going out with Kimi? Even if he's just looking for a hookup there's better options out there."

She was shocked by the way they insulted her.

"Right?"

"I even invited you along to the group date thinking you'd make a good match with him, you know."

"I don't know about that."

They still didn't realize Kimi was listening, so they said everything they wanted to.

"She was so down after the accident, but lately she's a lot better. Some girls just don't care about anyone but themselves. But who cares? At least we don't have to worry about her killing herself now. It'd look really bad if someone in our department killed themselves."

The two of them passed by. Kimi was left there twisting her

fingers around themselves nervously.

Kimi herself still wasn't sure why Nishiki wanted to go out with her. She thought there were better options too. She was no stranger to harsh self-criticism.

But the last thing that Itose had said wouldn't leave her mind.

Lately she's a lot better. The words weighed heavily on her.

"Kimi, what are you doing?" Nishiki asked, head tilted. She was still leaning against the tree.

"Oh, nothing," she said, looking up at him.

"Well, okay then. Do you have plans? Do you wanna come over to my place?"

"Sure," she said.

Kimi walked beside him. Sunlight filtered through the trees along the path, falling at their feet, and each time the trees were rocked by the wind, the light wavered. It was so beautiful it made her smile.

"Nice weather today," Nishiki said, looking up at the sky. *Sharing my feelings with you makes me happy—and sad.*

With him by my side, I can be positive as I deal with my painful memories. But I think about my family less and less. And it makes me feel heartless.

When they got to Nishiki's house, Kimi took the pastries she'd bought on campus out of her bag and they had a light snack. Nishiki had also bought some bread at a convenience store.

Unlike Kimi, who loved to try all sorts of new things, Nishiki didn't know much about food. He survived on simple meals—

simple enough to make Kimi worry that he wasn't getting enough vitamins.

Often the things he bought would end up expiring before he got around to eating them. Kimi had noticed food left in his refrigerator like an objet d'art time after time, which wasn't like him in many other ways.

"I'm going to the bathroom."

When he finished eating, Nishiki got up, put on some music, and went into the bathroom. She was sitting there listening to the music when he came back with a canned coffee in his hand. He always drank black coffee.

They kept talking for a while, but eventually Nishiki touched his hand to her cheek as if to stop her speaking. Kimi felt herself leaning into him.

I feel at ease when I'm with him.

She had often wondered why that might be. And the word that always came to mind was "boundaries." Just as he set his own boundaries, he never tried to cross over Kimi's impenetrable boundary—he had never asked about her family. He never spoke about his own family either.

Does he know not to go there? Or is it just a coincidence? Or—does he share the same pain?

When it was over, Nishiki took a sip of his coffee. Kimi looked up at him, wrapped in a blanket.

I want to be with him. But I can't forgive myself for trying to move on.

After the accident I wished that I had died with my family. I don't now.

Maybe if I had gone on the trip, my dad would've come to Tokyo to pick me up. He would've taken a different route. The timing would've been different. And my family wouldn't have been there at that moment, at that place where the accident happened.

It was a series of *what-ifs*. But those what-ifs appealed to her. She wondered if her own choice not to go had led to her family's death. So she could not forgive herself. *Not ever. . .*

"You have a nice name." The words took her aback.

"Huh?"

She looked back up at Nishiki, who was fumbling for words.

"It means 'precious future,' doesn't it?"

"My parents gave me one character each from their names. It wasn't really supposed to have a meaning." Before she would have easily explained.

But Nishiki's words had shaken her to her core.

Precious future. What my mother and father gave to me.

Until this moment, when she had remembered her family, she had pictured them as they were in the morgue. But now she saw them as they had been when they were alive.

Her father was grinning, her mother was smiling kindly, and her brother looked slightly fed up, but they all smiled as they looked at Kimi. Their eyes said to her that they would always be there, and encouraged her to hurry up and move on.

On to the precious future that her name suggested.

"What's wrong? Why are you crying?"

Kimi covered her face with her hands. "No," she said. But she couldn't stop crying.

All the guilt she was hanging on to, all the ways she'd been punishing herself, all of it slowly and quietly slipped away with her tears.

Thank you, Nishiki.

You saved my broken heart.

Thanks to you I'm still here, not lost forever. I want to be with you until you tell me to go away. No matter what happens, I want to be by your side.

This desire was the start of a painful pathway. But that made it no less colorful.

"Nishiki, you saved me . . . that's why I'm still here."

It's all right, I'm alive.

It doesn't matter who or what you are.

As long as you're you, that's fine with me.

A bridge between Ghouls and humanity.

#005 [MATCHING]

#006 [DEVIL APE]

I know. I know you all want to know about my past.

Once there was a group of Ghouls, based in the 20th Ward, that killed investigators in every ward. They wore big hoods and monkey masks with one fang sticking out, and they swung their Kagune around to show off their power.

In general, Ghouls are solitary creatures. Especially the stronger ones. But nevertheless the Apes were strong, and they were united as one. But their leader was the strongest of them all, the major power behind the Apes—Devil Ape.

Even with his monkey mask on he had incredible strength, and stealing people's lives was like a game to him. If his enemy was a good match, then he enjoyed himself even more.

The CCG took measures to combat the Apes, of course. In

particular, to try to destroy Devil Ape, who was the nucleus of the group, they tried to set a two- or three-layered net to catch him. But Devil Ape just slipped right through the net like their work was laughable to him.

The body count was ever growing. There was nothing for the CCG to do but to create a big, sweeping strategy. Talk had started going around stations about their plan.

And then Devil Ape suddenly disappeared.

Did he decide to hide out after hearing what the CCG was up to? Or did he die in a conflict with another Ghoul group? Everyone was speculating but the truth was not yet clear. Where had Devil Ape gone?

The answer lay within a coffee shop in the 20th Ward.

"Whoa, even dust runs in fear of the Devil Ape's fists!"

"Koma's got a mop in his hands. That's why the dust is going everywhere."

The man's name was Enji Koma. He had a big nose that made an impression, and small, round, sharp eyes. It would be beyond flattery to say that he had a nice appearance, but there was something charming about him anyway. He was the man they called Devil Ape, the one who was feared by CCG investigators.

And he was currently mopping floors in a café.

It had all begun when he met Yoshimura, the owner of the café. He had suddenly appeared to Koma and told him to end this futile conflict.

It took a real moron to try to tell Devil Ape what to do. Koma bared his fangs and told him he was going to regret that, but Yoshimura was prepared for this laughably quick rejection. Yoshimura had a rare spirit for a Ghoul.

What hit Koma next wasn't a Kagune, although he was prepared for a battle to the death.

"Let's just have a conversation, shall we?"

Yoshimura hit him with a gentle suggestion.

Yoshimura told him that he wanted to live in human society, without unnecessary killing. It was strange to wish for such a thing while holding the power of a Ghoul. But Koma found something strangely attractive about the idea. He wanted to try to see what Yoshimura wanted to see. So he decided to follow him. It is no exaggeration to say that this is where the second chapter of Koma's life began.

Next he came to Yoshimura's café, Anteiku. It was a café for both Ghouls and humans. They sold coffee, of course. One of the few things that could be shared by Ghouls and humans.

"Mr. Yoshimura, what can I do for you? Should I make coffee?" Koma asked excitedly, clad in a uniform. He'd never made coffee before, but he would try. His enthusiasm would have moved any living creature under the sun.

He didn't know how to act around humans, but he didn't imagine there was much interaction between a clerk and a customer anyway. Besides, he just wanted to make coffee. He wanted to make his debut as a master barista.

But Yoshimura handed him a mop and a bucket, two items that had nothing to do with coffee.

"But Mr. Yoshimura, this is . . ."

Never mind, he thought, *I can show off my creative dance skills with the mop and bucket, to bring in customers. It'll make me stand out, and people might like it too.*

But Yoshimura's reply was very simple.

"First I want you to clean the shop."

Koma's round eyes widened. *Cleaning is boring, shitty work that anyone can do. Is he really making Devil Ape do that?*

Once upon a time Koma would've killed him for the insult. But he realized something now: the real reason why Yoshimura had given him the task of cleaning.

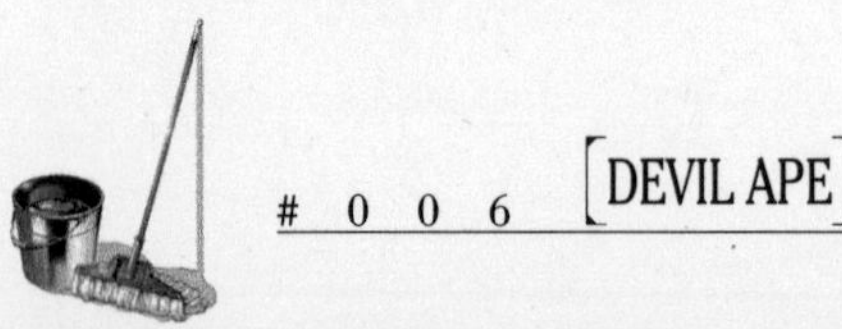

"Oh, yes, of course . . ."

Koma grinned and took the mop and bucket. "Got it!"

And he started cleaning, something he was unfamiliar with.

"Got a new guy working here?"

It wasn't long until the first customer of the day came in. She looked like a young office worker, stopping in on her way to work. Human. She looked at Koma with curiosity in her eyes.

It was a new expression for Koma, who was more used to seeing humans trembling in fear.

"Oh, pay no mind to me, miss," he said.

"Then quit swinging that mop around and splashing water everywhere! That shouldn't happen in a restaurant, you know, you should have your pay cut!"

Her response was cold. He immediately thought about killing her, but this was Yoshimura's place. Koma restrained himself and picked up the mop again.

"I'll have my usual," she said to Yoshimura, turning away from Koma quickly. There was nothing cute about this human.

Koma grew fonder of Yoshimura's way of life, but he still had absolutely no attachment to humans. *She doesn't deserve my special coffee*, he thought, and went back to cleaning. He decided to maintain indifference, but customers kept coming, one after another. First a man on his way to work, then an old lady who ran a sewing shop in the neighborhood, followed by a young man who stopped in by chance, and a woman who seemed to be Yoshimura's friend. There were both Ghouls and humans there. Ghouls and humans sat side by side, across tables from each other, simply spending their time as they pleased.

Koma watched all of this as he wiped down the window with spray and newspaper.

II

"Devil Ape! My brother! People are talking about you!"

He had been working at Anteiku for a few weeks. Whenever he saw a member of the Apes, they all looked very serious and said something similar.

"You guys know how Devil Ape always loves to be the center of attention!" Koma would tilt his head as if to suggest they must be confused about something, but then his friends would say, "Nah, man!"

"Can you believe Devil Ape's mopping the floors at Anteiku? Don't make me laugh!"

Everyone else would nod.

"I was ready to knock some heads for spreading that bullshit! But then I went down to Anteiku and saw him doing that shit myself... Our brother should not be sweeping a café floor!"

They could not control their anger. They stamped the ground.

"That bastard Yoshimura, making our brother work like that! He's got it coming!"

Their anger seemed to have turned on Yoshimura now. But

Koma looked at them sharply.

"Hey, don't talk bad about Yoshimura."

Koma's words only ratcheted up the tension. But he was glad to know that his comrades' feelings for him were still strong.

"But Devil Ape! My brother!"

Koma looked around at his former comrades, who had come here to beg and plead with him to return. After a long pause, he finally spoke.

"Do you guys know what 'baking soda' is?"

"Baking . . . soda?"

They all looked at each other.

"Is that one of those drinks humans like?"

No, that's just soda. But none of them were going to deliver the punchline. Koma continued.

"I thought so too at first, but actually, it's something else. It's a magical powder that gets rid of even the toughest grease stains."

They started to get excited.

"You mean those really sticky, greasy ones?!"

"Yeah. But that's not all. It also has a deodorizing effect, and it neutralizes the smell of sweat."

"Are you sayin' it fights stains and bad smells too?!"

"Yes, it also eliminates foot smells from your shoes."

"Even the smell of feet?!"

Several of them held up their feet. They seemed to know something about having smelly feet.

"Devil Ape, is this some kind of miracle drug?"

He looked at his comrades, in shock at all the things that baking soda could do, and he shook his head.

"Now this is the most surprising part. Humans can eat it."

"They can?!"

"That's right. There are different kinds of baking soda, and some of them are used in food."

He explained that it was what made pancakes fluffy, among other things. Ghouls had almost nothing to do with human foods, but everyone was still surprised by all that baking soda could do.

"Yoshimura told me all about it when I was trying to clean the ventilation fan with two feathers. And he originally learned about it from a human. I thought cleaning was a boring, pointless job too, at first. But there's a surprising amount to it. It's not as easy as it looks. And," he added, "I know some of you have been saying how horrible Yoshimura is for making me do the cleaning. But that's really just a mark of prestige for Anteiku and Yoshimura."

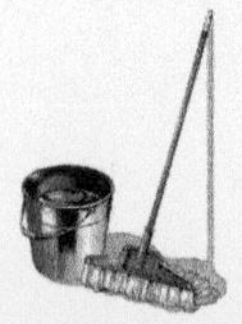

When Yoshimura had asked him to clean, Koma had freaked out. He thought that Yoshimura was sacrificing him to improve Anteiku's standing in the 20th Ward.

"It's true, Devil Ape, our brother. Everyone thinks Yoshimura's a real bastard . . ."

"I know. If one of these other Ghouls who only care about looking cool were in my position, there's no way in hell they'd do it. But I'm not like that. Mr. Yoshimura trusted me with this mission. This kind of dirty work is no big deal."

His spirit of self-sacrifice was moving. The other Apes were impressed.

"You're a good guy, my brother! Still out there doing battle, just with stubborn grease stains!"

Tears fell from his comrades' eyes as they lamented their own lack of maturity and forward thinking. One clapped Koma on the shoulder.

"Does baking soda do anything for ape tears?"

It was a joke meant to make everyone feel better. And it worked; everyone smiled.

"You don't have an enemy in the world, my brother!"

III

"Cleaning again?" laughed the young lady who looked like she worked in an office, seeing Koma out sweeping in front of the café again. Koma had worked at Anteiku for a few months now, and he always started the day by cleaning.

"Oops, you caught me. Morning, Tsubasa. You're sharp as ever today."

"And you're as thickheaded as ever today, Koma. All you can do is clean . . . is what I'd like to say, but actually, it's pretty nice to watch you when you're at it."

Although leaves from the trees along the road were everywhere, there were none in front of Anteiku. But the outside of the café wasn't the only thing that was spotless—the inside was too. It gleamed thanks to Devil Ape's special cleaning techniques.

Koma, who had been cleaning ever since he was first entrusted with the task, had become better at it than any army of housewives or professional cleaners.

"It looks like you just tipped a bucket of water on the floor, but that can't be true."

"Oh, Tsubasa, don't tell me you want to know my secrets."

"I don't care."

"No need to restrain yourself!"

"Oh, Mr. Koma, enough already!"

Her words were stinging but the expression on her face was joyful. She looked like she enjoyed talking to Koma.

"Oh, and you polished everything today, too!"

And Tsubasa wasn't the only one who liked to talk to him. Many customers at Anteiku would seek him out for a conversation.

"All the coffee cups should be much shinier today."

"Oh, I must pay attention to my cup, then."

"Be on the lookout!"

She laughed.

This human, who would've been terrified of Koma before, actually smiled at him now. And she told him things. About her family, work, school. She had a lot of stories about things Ghouls could never experience.

And so, eventually, Koma was not the only one who could meet humans naturally.

"My brother! With everything you taught me I got a part-time job of my own!"

Now the rest of the Apes could too.

"I have to clean up at work too, but I'm really not any good at it. So everyone helped me! And while we were talking we really hit it off! I mean, I can't go out for food or drinks with them but it's still fun!"

They all seemed to have been inspired by seeing their leader, Devil Ape, sweating and working his fingers to the bone.

The Apes, who had the strongest sense of togetherness of all the Ghoul groups, had followed a strict hierarchy that served them well in human society.

And as they got to know people more their knowledge grew.

Some of these discoveries shocked Koma.

But then the next blow was lessened, and the next, until it was just a minor reverberation in his stomach. Sometimes the pain rose up within him and made his chest ache.

"Those Ghouls are at it again . . . better be careful out there," Tsubasa said looking up at the TV as she drank the coffee that came with her breakfast as usual one morning. Koma was usually talkative, but at those moments he never knew what to say.

"Getting sentimental in my old age . . ."

When his shift was over, Koma changed out of his uniform alone, lost in thought. There was a pall hanging over him that he could not shake off. *This isn't like me,* he thought. *But wait. Do I need to shake this feeling off in the first place?*

"Mr. Koma . . ." He heard a soft voice behind him.

"Mr. Yoshimura." Koma turned around.

"Do you have a moment?"

"For you, Mr. Yoshimura, I would go anywhere or do anything," he said lightheartedly, forcing himself to cheer up. Yoshimura led the way.

They went into the café. The place looked sad with nobody in it. *No, I'm the one who's sad when nobody's in there.*

"Have a seat."

Yoshimura gestured toward the seats at the counter. Once Koma sat down, Yoshimura went into the kitchen and started making coffee.

"How's work treating you, Mr. Koma?"

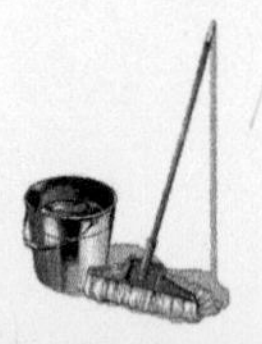

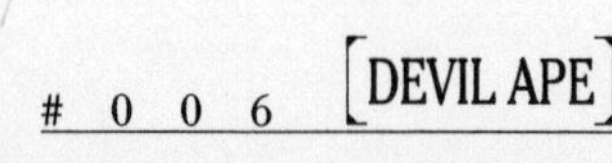

"The dust is so afraid of my cleaning it hardly shows its face around here anymore!" Koma always loved to exaggerate. Yoshimura nodded in agreement.

"You clean so well every day that it's always sparkling in here."

Yoshimura set a cup of coffee down in front of Koma. The steam rising off of it brought the rich aroma to his nostrils. When Koma thought about it, he realized that he'd never relaxed and enjoyed a cup of coffee in his life.

"Here at Anteiku we're all friends, and helping each other out is our motto," Yoshimura mumbled as Koma picked up his cup of coffee. "And you're being helped," he said, then fell silent.

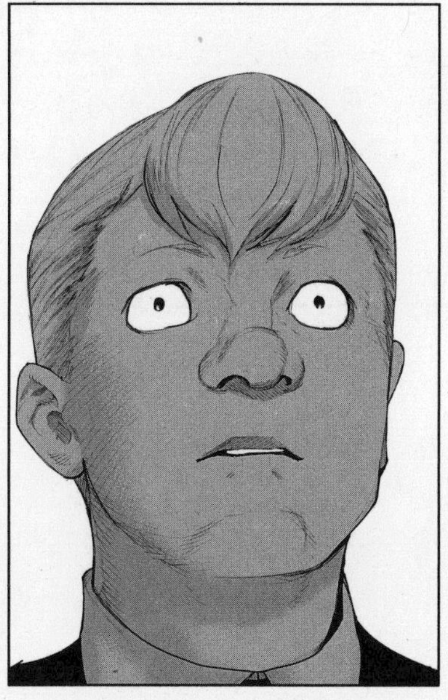

Yoshimura seemed to have picked up on Koma's conflict. Perhaps he knew the reason, the cause, everything. And perhaps he shared the same pain, despite his desire to coexist with humans.

Koma took a gulp of the coffee Yoshimura had made for him. And as he drank he gave into the warmth of the steam, and realized he was about to cry.

"This Devil Ape will do his best to help you from here on,

Mr. Yoshimura. It would be my honor."

Yoshimura smiled softly.

"Then you'd better get started learning how to make coffee."

"Coffee?!"

Koma jumped to his feet, taken off guard by this unexpected proposal. Koma had dedicated himself to cleaning and now saw the art of coffee making as something in the realm of the gods. It was something special that not just anybody could do.

"You know, Tsubasa whispered to me the other day, 'I wish I could try Mr. Koma's coffee.' "

Surely this wasn't the same Tsubasa who always insulted him.

"I've had other customers ask about you as well."

Anteiku, where friends help each other out. How broadly was the term "friend" defined?

"So I can't let down those customers who want to try Devil Ape's coffee!"

Each of them could have pointed at the other if they were asked to say which one wanted to help and which one needed to be helped.

From that day, Yoshimura started teaching Koma to make coffee. How to roast the beans, how to pour the hot water—every step had a role in making great coffee. After each lesson, Koma practiced what Yoshimura had taught him on his own, and he also made coffee for the other Apes.

Then, finally, the day came. Tsubasa entered the shop as usual to find Koma behind the counter, waiting.

"What's going on? The cleaner's behind the counter!"

"I thought we'd have Mr. Koma help us out making coffee from now on," said Yoshimura.

"What? Don't tell me he sloshes coffee around like he does that mop bucket." As she grumbled, Tsubasa took her seat and asked for a cup of coffee, "made by Mr. Koma."

"Coming right up!"

Coffee is a delicate thing. I don't understand everything that goes into it myself. It's just detailed procedure after detailed procedure. But that's pretty much what it takes for Ghouls and humans to live together.

"Enjoy," he said, setting the cup down. *A cup full of passion.*

"This better be good," Tsubasa teased him as she picked up the coffee and brought it to her lips. The coffee swelled over her lips and disappeared over her tongue. "It is."

These two honest words fell from her lips, which usually had nothing but poison on them.

Naturally Koma felt pride that the coffee he'd made was good, but to hear those words from her gave him a feeling of excitement.

Tsubasa smiled and looked happy. A smile from a customer—and a human. It looked like a dazzling light, and it made him unbearably happy, as well as hurting him tremendously.

The more Koma got to know people, the more this feeling sprouted in him, and the more he understood the root of this pain.

Light not only illuminates all creatures, but it also casts shadows. And those shadows also tell of all the crimes I have committed.

The more he started to like humans, the more he realized just what he'd done to them in the past.

He remembered people who had fallen to the ground, screaming, "I have kids, I have a family, I don't want to die, help me!"

There were people who had confronted him so their friends could escape.

I wonder if they had a nice life like this. If they had happy moments. The pain grabbed at his insides ruthlessly.

I met Mr. Yoshimura and he got me thinking about wanting to live with humans. But I don't think I have the right to live with them. These two conflicting feelings pushed up against each other, colliding within him, and the impact was hard to bear.

"Mr. Koma? Mr. Koma?"

He realized he was standing there, frozen. Tsubasa kept saying his name in a confused way.

"Oh, sorry. I was just overwhelmed by emotion there."

"Overwhelmed by your own coffee? You are a strange one."

Tsubasa looked amazed but she smiled nonetheless. Other regulars who came in after her also found Koma standing behind the counter, and they joked about how he'd finally graduated from cleaning.

These shadows, these things he did in the past, would continue to cause him pain. He still wasn't sure whether living was atonement for them, or if death would be a better atonement. All he could do was try to understand the magnitude of the crimes he had committed.

I need time to think. So just for now I'm going to keep on living. Those shadows may bring me suffering, but I want to see all the

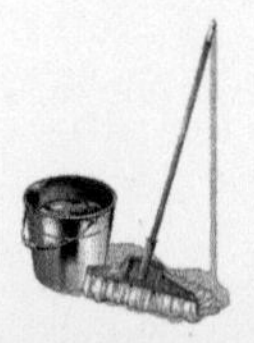

brightly colored, blossoming things this world has to offer that I've never seen before.

VI

Shortly after, someone new came to the café. It was Kaya Irimi, the leader of the Black Dobers.

"No way will we ever work together, Irimi."

"Shut up, monkey boy."

Like the Apes, the infamous Black Dobers had also caught the attention of the CCG, and their leader had decided to come to Anteiku too. *What on earth is happening?*

Although their exchange was playful, Koma was her superior now. He imagined Irimi would start off doing the cleaning too. A strange emotion came over him when he imagined the leader of the Black Dobers, famous for her insistence on total obedience, slinging a mop around.

"Well, then, Kaya, first let's learn how to make a cup of coffee."

But Yoshimura's words shocked Koma. Why was Yoshimura teaching her how to make coffee when she'd just gotten here? And on top of that, he served it to someone straight away.

"Irimi's coffee is the best."

"Somehow a woman's touch is just better."

All the male customers adored her. Even Tsubasa loved her. When she'd heard recently that Irimi had a boyfriend, she and Irimi started joking around. "If we have a boy, I'll name him Shota."

And with Irimi there, Koma no longer had a place behind the counter, and cleaning duty fell back to him again.

"You've been working at Anteiku for so long, and the leader of the Black Dobers just waltzes right into the kitchen, my brother!"

As long as Ghouls were coming into the café, rumors were quick to get around. His comrades from the Apes who heard about what was going on at Anteiku were once again incensed on his behalf. Especially because it involved the Black Dobers.

Also, since they'd all been inspired to find their own jobs, they often tried to turn the conversation into a passionate discussion about concrete problems they were facing, like issues with their contracts. But Koma would just smile and say, "You don't understand. This isn't a work issue, it's a matter of the heart."

"Irimi is not like me, she's very immature. Which makes it hard for me to understand the intention behind Mr. Yoshimura's actions.

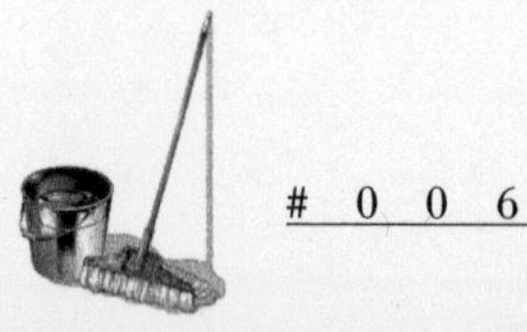

But perhaps he hopes that being in the kitchen straightaway will make her grow up a little and step up to the plate."

As Koma spoke he saw that it was true—that Irimi had been put into the kitchen because she was being evaluated.

"Of course!"

"My brother, you're amazing!" The Apes cheered.

Whatever position Yoshimura puts me in, I will not complain. I will do my best. That's what makes me a man.

And besides, there are people watching.

"Mr. Koma, you're so amazing. Whatever you do you give it your all," Tsubasa whispered to him one day as he was in front of the café, engaged in his age-old battle with the fallen leaves.

"Really? Looks pointless to me," said Irimi.

"Well, that too!" agreed Tsubasa, before giving her order to Irimi. "But he used to be so bad at cleaning, and now he's a pro. And the coffee he makes is great. Just watching him work is more fun than anything. It just makes me happy every morning."

Tsubasa smiled and put her finger to her lips, as if to tell Irimi to be careful not to tell Koma. When she saw that smile, Irimi listened. Koma darted here and there as he pursued the fallen leaves, until the path was perfectly clear. Devil Ape, the Ghoul once feared by all investigators, now focused all his attention on cleaning, something Irimi said was worthless.

But Irimi did not make fun of him.

He is practicing coexistence with humans. And winning their trust. I can't let him beat me.

He set a good example for her. Because Yoshimura trusted him to do what needed to be done.

"Are you ready for the Devil Ape rolling hurricane?!"

Anteiku would be gleaming today, too.

And it would be until the end.

"Mr. Yoshimura, I gave it the old Devil Ape Special Cleaning Service! Nice and shiny."

We're all friends at Anteiku, and we help each other.

Now to prove it.

TOKYO
GHOUL

Thank you for picking up the third novel. I believe this will be the final one in the series. I would like to thank Mr. Towada for writing them, the editor, Mr. 65, and everyone who has read these novels. Whatever comes next, I hope you'll be with me for that too.

Sui

Finally, the third part of the novelization. Although he was busy writing *Tokyo Ghoul: Zakki*, Mr. Ishida kindly took the time to check everything in these novelizations too. I must give my thanks to Mr. Ishida for his passion, and to the fans for their love for the series. Thank you very much.

Shin Towada